***Beck wanted t[...]
was going to b[...]***

He'd be lying if he d[...]
hostage incident did[...] the SWAT
team busted in.

In fact, Jennifer Barclay's wide brown eyes told
him shock had inched its way in, forcing into her
eyes the kind of glazed disbelief he'd seen too
many times. She'd been stronger than most, but
that was over.

It was a mistake of monumental proportions and
he knew it, but Beck decided he didn't care. He
reached for her.

She stepped back so quickly she almost fell.
Grabbing the window sill, she spoke from
between gritted teeth. 'You lied to me! You
promised no one would get hurt.'

Immediately, Beck's mask slid into place. Her
words weren't what he'd expected, but different
people reacted in different ways. Jennifer had
been holding her emotions in check for hours
and now she was going to erupt. At him.

She made no attempt to hide her emotions,
and it wouldn't have mattered if she had. He
understood better than she did what she
was feeling.

*I feel guilty because I couldn't stop this. I feel guilty
because I survived.*

Dear Reader,

Welcome to Superromance.

This is a month of real variety, where your choices go from heart-warming novels to stories that will set your heart pounding. For instance, *The Negotiator* from Kay David is the first in a set of three books based around a police SWAT team, THE GUARDIANS, and it's vivid, fascinating & action-packed reading.

Brenda Novak returns with another NINE MONTHS LATER tale, *Snow Baby*, a dramatic, emotional story that starts with a heroic rescue and a night of passion, but covers so much more…

A self-made millionaire who is out for revenge gives relatively new author Kathleen O'Brien's *A Self-Made Man* its glamorous starting point, while *White Picket Fences* from Tara Taylor Quinn returns to the Shelter Valley community, where everyone knows and cares about each other, for another of this author's deeply felt stories of romance and family.

Enjoy them all,

The Editors

The Negotiator

KAY DAVID

™ SILHOUETTE®
SUPERROMANCE™

First published in Great Britain 2002
Silhouette Books, Eton House, 18-24 Paradise Road,
Richmond, Surrey TW9 1SR

© Carla Luan 2001

ISBN 0 373 70960 9

38-0702

Printed and bound in Spain
by Litografia Rosés S.A., Barcelona

Dear Reader,

Thirty-five years ago this August, I was eleven years old. Sitting in the front seat of my mother's Cadillac, I waited impatiently for my eighteen-year-old sister Dana while she purchased petrol. It was unbearably hot and I was already upset. In just a few weeks, Dana was moving away from home, going to Austin and the University of Texas. She was growing up and leaving me behind.

Then the radio blared with a sudden bulletin. That didn't happen quite so often in those days as it does now, and even my young ears perked up as the announcer began to speak with anxious excitement. His news was not good.

A sniper was in the clock tower at the university, and he was shooting people. In broad daylight. With a high-powered rifle. I yelled at my sister to come quick and listen. We sat in the sweltering heat of that August day and held our breath. As the news went on, seemingly forever, her eyes met mine, a mixture of horror, disbelief and fright darkening their depths.

By the end of that afternoon, Charles Whitman had shot over forty people, killing more than a dozen strangers, plus his wife and mother. The rest of us were wounded, too, because he taught us a terrible lesson that day. No one is safe.

That incident is largely regarded as the genesis for SWAT teams as we know them. Back then, law enforcement officials weren't prepared; they'd encountered few situations like this. Today, unfortunately, we're all much better equipped, physically if not emotionally, to deal with such horrible circumstances. Daily, SWAT teams the world over handle hostage situations, suicide threats, snipers…anything and everything that is dangerous and deadly.

The Negotiator is the first in a trilogy of books I've written about just such a team. It will be followed in August and September by *The Commander* and *The Listener*. Set in the Florida panhandle, each of these stories will focus on a special member of the team. No one can fully understand the stress and danger these brave men and women face every day. I hope in some small way, however, that I've deepened understanding for everything they—and the people who love them—do to keep the rest of us safe.

Sincerely,

Kay David

This book is dedicated to the incredibly brave police officers who struggle every day to make the world a safer place. Their jobs are too important and too dangerous for any writer to fully capture the essence of their sacrifices, but I hope these stories somehow express the appreciation I feel for their efforts.

A special acknowledgement to Laura and Paula. Your support and encouragement mean more than I can adequately express. Thank you both for having faith in my abilities and for giving me the opportunity to tell the stories my way.

CHAPTER ONE

Looking back on it, that night after everything was over, Jennifer Barclay realized with amazement that the morning had started out like any other ordinary day.

She'd had no sense of impending doom, no feeling things were about to go horribly wrong. Not a single clue. If she'd known—if she'd had even the slightest inkling—she would have stayed home in bed.

But she hadn't suspected a thing.

She'd arrived at Westside Elementary at seven-thirty and by four that afternoon, as usual, she was totally exhausted. She loved her job as a fourth-grade teacher, but by May, even she needed a break. With only another five weeks of school, the kids had been wild, and none of them had wanted to concentrate. Their heads were at the coast, a mile down Highway 98, where the white Florida sand and crashing emerald waves were just begging to be enjoyed. Truth be told, Jennifer had had a hard time focusing herself…but for a totally different reason.

She'd had to change her schedule.

Jennifer always visited her mother on Wednesdays

and Saturdays, but this afternoon she wouldn't be able to make it to the nursing home. She'd had to arrange an after-school meeting for the children participating in the annual beach cleanup, and the disruption to her usual orderly agenda bothered her a lot. Her friends teased her, but for Jennifer, routine meant everything. During her childhood, no plans had ever been made, much less kept, and now nothing was more important to her than the steady, day-to-day patterns she lived by.

She hurried down the hallway toward her class-room and tried to convince herself to stop worrying. Half the time Nadine Barclay didn't even know who she was, never mind if Jennifer was there or not. Alzheimer's had robbed Jennifer's mother of her family and her memories. Jennifer wanted to be a good daughter to her mother, though. She showed up twice a week whether Nadine knew it or not.

Whether Jennifer wanted to or not.

Reaching her classroom, she walked inside and closed the door behind her. In between the last bell and the scheduled meeting, she had exactly five minutes to gulp the diet cola she'd retrieved from the teachers' lounge, but she hadn't even taken her first sip when the door opened. She closed her eyes for just a second, then turned to see who was standing in the doorway.

Ten-year-old Juan Canales smiled shyly at her.

"Juan!" Putting aside her plans to snatch a moment of peace, Jennifer grinned and held up the icy drink. "Come on in. I just went and got a Coke. If you don't tell anyone, I'll share it with you!"

He replaced his indecisive look with one of contained excitement. His family was very poor, and she doubted he and his siblings got enough to eat. Sodas would have been out of the question. The Canales family represented the flip side of Destin, the beautiful resort town Westside Elementary served. Juan's mother cleaned rooms for one of the elegant beach hotels and his father clipped the bushes surrounding its luxurious pool. When Jennifer handed the little boy the filled paper cup, he gripped it with two hands and sipped slowly.

Jennifer studied Juan surreptitiously as he drank. He was one of her very best students, and even though she knew she wasn't supposed to have favorites, Jennifer had to admit, he was one. Smart, clever and as sweet as he could be, Juan Canales made Jennifer ache to have children of her own. He was a perfect example of why she'd become a teacher, too. He seemed as starved for information as he was for everything else.

He finished his drink with noisy gusto and she poured the last of the Coke into his cup with a smile.

"I wasn't all that thirsty," she confided. "I'm glad you're here to help me."

His eyes rounded with pleasure. "*Muchas gra-*

cias…uh…thank you very much, Miss Barclay. It really tastes good.''

Within a few minutes, a dozen other ten-year-olds had arrived, and Jennifer started passing out permission slips. She walked up and down the aisle between the desks and spoke. "I have to have these back by next week, signed, sealed and delivered. You can't participate in the beach cleanup if I don't have this on record, okay?" Returning to the front of the room, she stopped beside her desk and rested one hip on the corner. "We're cleaning up at Blue Mountain. Does everyone know where that is?"

The question prompted chatter and Jennifer grinned, letting it wash over her. God, she loved her job! The students, their enthusiasm, their joy— they represented everything good in her life. Actually, they represented *everything* in her life. Even her free hours were devoted to the school and if she wasn't visiting her mother, she was here.

Again, sometimes she took ribbing over this. "There's more to living than just work," her best friend Wanda would say. The black woman, who was Nadine's nurse, constantly gave Jennifer a hard time. She was right, of course, but Jennifer had her life organized just as she liked it.

She held up her hands for silence, but before she could speak, she heard a noise in the hallway. Jennifer glanced curiously at the door and the small window in the upper half.

Howard French stood before the glass. The strained expression on the young man's face brought Jennifer to her feet, bells of warning sounding inside her head. He'd been fired from the maintenance staff just last week. What on earth was he doing here now?

Starting toward the door, she thought of how she'd tried to help him. She'd complained after he'd been let go, but it'd been pointless, and she'd known that before she stepped inside Betty Whitmire's office. The school's local board member, Betty hated the simple man. More than once, Jennifer had cringed, hearing Betty's stinging voice down the hall. "If you can't do better than that, French, we'll find someone who can. Mopping the floor isn't brain surgery, you know!"

Jennifer was halfway to the door when Howard burst inside. He stumbled once, then straightened, giving his arm a short jerk. A screaming woman lurched in behind him, her hands on her head in a useless attempt to ease the grip Howard had on her hair. He turned and locked the door behind him, pulling the shade down with his other hand. For a moment, the scene made no sense, no sense at all, then the woman shrieked again, and things became distressingly clear. Disheveled and obviously distraught, Betty Whitmire had an ugly bruise on the side of her face and a rip in the sleeve of her dress. Jennifer's heart stopped, then leapt inside her chest and began to pound, disbelief leaving her mouth dry.

She spoke without thinking. "Howard? My God—what's going on? Wh-what are you doing with Mrs. Whitmire?"

He didn't answer, and Betty's labored breathing was raw and guttural in the shocked hush of the room. Behind Jennifer, one of the children started to sniffle. The sound seemed to bring Howard out of his apparent trance.

"You got to help me, Miss Jennifer," he cried. "I'm in trouble."

Not knowing what else to do, Jennifer took two steps toward the crazed man and his hostage.

"Don't come no further!" he screamed. "Don't do it!"

She wanted to argue, but nothing came out. She was paralyzed, and all she could do was stare as he swung up the barrel of a rifle and pointed it directly at her.

THE DUFFEL BAG was already strained at the seams when Beck Winters threw in one more book, then yanked the zipper closed. He was taking his first vacation in eight years and he wasn't really sure what people did on vacation. He wanted to have plenty to read in case he got bored. He just couldn't stand having time on his hands and nothing to do. His brain would sense the emptiness and before he could stop it, his thoughts would take him places he didn't want to go.

Looking around one more time, he walked out of the bedroom. He was almost to the front door when the telephone rang. As if getting a reprieve, he dropped the bag and raced into the kitchen. "Beck Winters," he answered eagerly.

"We've got a call." Lena McKinney's throaty voice filled the line. The SWAT team's lieutenant, Lena kept the two cells of the group organized and motivated as they covered the Emerald Coast of Florida from just past Pensacola all the way down to Panama City Beach. The fifteen members were close as a family, albeit a dysfunctional one at times.

"I know you're about to leave but Bradley's got the flu and he's whining like a baby. But he couldn't work this one even if he felt okay. We're at Westside Elementary. Get here as fast as you can. We've got a man gone barricade. There are hostages, too."

Beck didn't bother to ask any questions because Lena hung up before he could voice them, just as he'd known she would. If she was there and had called him, the team was already on-site with the perimeter secured and a sniper in place. Now they needed someone to talk. A negotiator. Kicking the duffel aside, Beck ran out the front door without wasting another minute. It'd been planned for a long time, but obviously his vacation would just have to wait.

Thank God...

He hadn't a clue what to do with himself anyway.

"HOWARD…" Jennifer made her voice as soft and nonthreatening as she could. "What's going on? Why do you have a gun? Why are you hurting Mrs. Whitmire like that?"

He looked at the woman whose hair he still held. He almost seemed surprised to see her. Jerking his head up, he met Jennifer's gaze, his eyes wide and confused, his hand trembling on the weapon. "She was ugly to me," he said simply.

"That doesn't mean you have to be the same way to her." Jennifer held out her hands. "Put the rifle down, please, Howard. It's scaring the children."

The gun stayed level as he glanced behind her. Jennifer tried not to look down the barrel but she couldn't help herself. She felt her eyes go inexorably to the bore, and for just a second, black dots swam before her. She was a child herself, ten years old, terrified and helpless. Her vision tunneled, bloody images hovering on the edges like the ghosts they were.

Howard's voice yanked her back. "I—I don't care," he said. "N-nobody cares about me so why should I care about them?"

"That's not true, Howard. I care about you and so does everyone—"

"He's insane!" Betty Whitmire cried. Her voice was shrill and discordant, destroying Jennifer's effort for calmness like a train whistle shattering the night's silence. "He grabbed me in the hall and dragged me in here. He's going to kill us all!"

Jennifer stared at her in disbelief, wondering—not for the first time—how on earth the woman had managed to land her position on the school board. Her people skills were nonexistent, and she was totally clueless when it came to the kids. Neither the parents nor teachers respected her, but Jennifer had to admit one thing: Betty was involved. There wasn't a detail about any of the schools she didn't know.

Hearing Betty speak, one of the children started crying in earnest, small terrified sobs escaping. Jennifer turned and tried to look reassuring, but when she saw them, she wanted to cry herself. They'd fled their desks and had instinctively huddled at the back of the room. Cherise was the one sobbing, and Juan was patting her awkwardly on the arm, whispering something to her. His best friend, Julian, hovered nearby, an uncertain expression on his face. Jennifer caught Juan's eye and nodded slightly, hoping her approval would make its way across the room.

Looking at Howard once more, Jennifer spoke above the pounding of her heart. She made her words sound certain and composed, even though she was panicking inside. "Betty, please stay quiet. You're not helping matters. Howard is *not* going to shoot you. Not you, not anyone. Isn't that right, Howard? In fact, he's going to turn you loose right now."

He tightened his grip on Betty's scalp, but then unexpectedly opened his fist. She cried out and fell down, unprepared for the sudden release. From the

floor, she shot Jennifer a look of confusion mixed
with gratitude, then she scrambled past her on all
fours, heading for the children. Jennifer didn't turn
but she could hear the chairs scraping and the muffled
voices as they moved to accommodate her.

Taking advantage of the confusion, Jennifer forced
herself to move an inch nearer the man and the gun,
a trickle of sweat forming along her shoulders then
drawing a line down her back. She was lucky enough
to have a phone in her room, but there was no way
she could get to it and dial for help. Howard stood
between her and the wall where it hung.

She truly was confident that Howard wouldn't
shoot. He just wasn't that kind of man. When the
class hamster had died, he'd cried more than any of
the kids. If anything, he was too quiet and unassum-
ing…and every time she looked at him, Jennifer saw
her brother. Unlike Howard, Danny had been brilliant,
but in their eyes lived the same haunted expression.
It was filled with confusion, uncertainty and a complete lack of self-confidence. She'd been trying to
help the janitor since the day she'd met him. A pen-
ance, she knew.

Even still, a thousand thoughts crowded Jennifer's
head. Could she grab the gun? Should she even try?
What would happen if she didn't? Her forward movement finally registered and Howard yanked the
weapon up, tucking the stock under his arm.

"Don't come no closer, Miss Jennifer. I mean it. I'm serious."

Her mouth felt full of beach sand, but she held out her hands and spoke in an appeasing way. "Okay, okay, I'll stay right here. But talk to me. Tell me what's going on."

The air seemed to go out of his body and he slumped against her desk. The black, empty barrel of the rifle remained pointed at Jennifer's chest. "I'm in trouble," he said again. "Big, big trouble."

Another child started to cry. "Let the kids go, Howard," she whispered. "Let Mrs. Whitmire take them out and then you and I can talk. You can tell me what happened."

He shook his head morosely. "I can't let 'em go," he said. "I can't. It's too late."

"Too late for what?"

He shook his head and said nothing. The bore of the weapon dropped an inch.

"How can I help you if you won't tell me what's going on?" she asked. "Let them go. I'll stay. I promise."

"Won't do no good. Not now. Everbody hates me and they all think I'm stupid. It's too late." He dipped his head and shook it again, the picture of total dejection. "They hate me. All of 'em."

The gun slipped a second inch lower. Jennifer licked her lips, swallowed hard then took a quiet step forward. Another foot and she could touch the barrel, grab it, twist it away from him. She held her breath, trapping it inside her chest and holding it captive, afraid to even breathe. Slowly, so slowly the movement was practically imperceptible, she began to raise her right hand. Howard continued to talk.

"It's all wrong," he mumbled. "All wrong. I'm not that way. I'm a nice person. I really am."

Without any warning, he looked up. Jennifer stopped instantly, her hand halfway up her side. He didn't even seem to notice. "I'm a nice person," he cried. "I'm nice!"

"I know that," she said soothingly. "I know you are, Howard." Her shoulders tightened, a reflexive action. "But nice people don't point guns. So why don't you hand it over and we'll talk?" She took another step and reached out, her fingers brushing the cold, hard metal of the barrel.

She didn't know what happened first—the ringing phone or Howard's reaction—but an instant later, the opportunity was lost. Wild-eyed, he grabbed her and pulled her close.

"THEY'RE NOT ANSWERING." Beck turned to Lena and shook his head, the phone pressed to his ear. They were inside the War Wagon, a modified Winnebago motor home stocked with the equipment and supplies that would be required during any situation. Parked down the block from the school, he could see the side of the building, an older structure with tilt-out windows facing a worn playground. They were less than a mile from some of the most expensive real estate in Florida, but no one would know it from looking at the school. There was a world of difference between its run-down appearance and the elegant high-rises that dotted the sparkling beaches.

"Are you sure the phone's right there in her classroom? We never had phones inside the rooms when I was in school. Maybe I should drag out the bullhorn."

Lena stared at him, her gray eyes impatient and stormy as usual. "Wake up, Beck. This is the computer age. A lot of the classrooms have their own phones now. Besides that, the guys are already in place in the hallway and they can hear it ringing. It's the right phone."

"Maybe he took 'em somewhere else."

"They're there. A teacher saw the suspect grab a member of the school board who happened to be in the hall and drag her inside a classroom. She's pretty sure she saw a gun, but isn't positive. The responding officers didn't even try to go in. They just called us."

"How many are inside?"

"We don't know yet. Another teacher was having a meeting with some of the students. Fourth graders. Their teacher's name is Jennifer Barclay."

He gripped the phone tightly. He'd faced countless calls like this one since he'd joined the team, but Beck never did it without nervousness sucker punching him in the gut, especially if there were kids involved. He knew too much, he thought all at once. When he was less experienced and more reckless, he hadn't understood what was on the line.

Now he understood all too well.

He forced himself to focus. "Any background info yet?"

"Sarah's working on it, but she hasn't found a lot yet."

Beck nodded. The only nontactical member of the team, Sarah Greenberg served as the information officer. She labored just as hard and was just as sharp as any of the other cops. Her job was to gather any details they might need to resolve a situation. Next to time, information was key.

"Who's in there?"

Lena spoke as she brought a pair of high-powered binoculars to her eyes. "Cal and Jason are inside at one end of the hallway, and the rest of the gang's at the other end. We don't have much recon yet—can't see inside. The perp pulled the shade on the window in the door and apparently they're nowhere near the only window in the classroom. I've got the floor plans to the school and the guys have those already. Randy's across the street."

"Where?"

She nodded toward the row of the small frame houses opposite the school. "There, the fifth one down with the green shutters, the two-story with the oleanders in front. The owners are gone. Neighbor had a key and she let us in the back door.'' She handed Beck the glasses. ''He's in the upstairs corner window.''

Beck stared through the lenses and the head of Randy Tamirisa, the team's countersniper, leapt into focus. He was lying motionless behind his weapon, the sight trained on the school. Beck couldn't see his face, but he didn't need to. Black hair and even blacker eyes, Randy was an enigma to Beck, the exact opposite of most snipers. They'd never gotten along; hotheaded and heavy-handed, Randy didn't have the discipline Beck felt was necessary to be on the team, but Lena disagreed and she was the boss. Randy's perfect shooting range score didn't hurt, either.

''Where's Chase?''

Beside him Lena sighed.

''I know, I know—'' He spoke before she could answer him. ''Chase is not a member of my cell, and Randy is good, and what's my problem?'' He lowered the glasses and looked at the woman beside him.

''And the answer is?'' she said dryly.

''I don't trust Randy,'' he said bluntly, bringing the glasses back to his face. ''He's not a team player. He's a hot dog.''

''C'mon, Beck. He's been with us a year and he scores one hundred percent every time he's on the range. He's inexperienced but he's done nothing wrong.''

"He's done nothing period."

"Give the guy a chance. You were young once, too, you know."

"I was never that young." Without waiting for her reply, he picked up the phone and hit the redial button. It began to ring in his ear as he looked down at his boss. "I don't trust him," he repeated darkly, "and neither should you."

"LET ME ANSWER the phone, Howard, please." His arm was so tightly pressed against her throat, Jennifer could hardly speak. "P-please. I-it could be important."

"Who is it?" he asked illogically.

"I—I don't know." She put her fingers against his sleeve and gently tugged, trying for a little more air. He had on an orange jumpsuit, the uniform of the maintenance people. It smelled like diesel and fear. "Please, Howard."

They stood together in the center of the room. When the phone stopped ringing, the thick tension seemed to hold the vibrations. A moment later, the sound started all over just as it had for the past hour.

"Let me answer it," she whispered. "It might be a parent. Whoever it is won't give up."

"All right...but don't tell 'em anything. Don't tell 'em 'bout me."

They stumbled together toward the telephone, which hung on the wall beside the door. Jennifer's voice was breathless as she answered, and she prayed someone she knew was on the other end. Someone who could tell something was wrong with her even if she couldn't get the words out. "H-hello?"

"This is Officer Beck Winters with the Emerald Coast SWAT team. Who am I speaking with, please?"

Jennifer's heart knocked against her ribs in surprise, then she pulled herself together, fear, shock and relief combining inside her in a crazy mix. "Th-this is Jennifer Barclay."

"Who is it?"

"Is everyone okay in there?"

Howard's voice was harsh in her left ear, the policeman's cool tones were in her right. She answered the policeman and ignored Howard. "W-we're fine."

Howard jerked his arm and Jennifer gasped automatically. "Who is it?" His voice dropped and menace filled it. "You tell me who that is. Right now!"

Jennifer turned slightly and looked into his face. Their eyes were inches apart, and she'd never noticed until this moment that one of his irises was lighter than the other. For some unexplained reason, those mismatched eyes sparked a moment of fear. She spoke quickly. "It's the police. They want to know if everyone's okay."

His reaction was the last one she expected. He stiffened, dropped his arm from her neck and slowly began to back up, shaking his head. The rifle stayed pointed at her.

"Miss Barclay? Jennifer? Talk to me. I need to know what's going on."

Her mind drifting strangely, she imagined what the cop must look like—he had to be a big man, tall and barrel-chested, judging from the depth of his voice. Dark hair, she decided, and a pleasant face, rounded and caring.

"What does he want?" Howard asked again.

Apparently hearing the question, the cop spoke, still composed, still collected. He could have been asking to speak to his own brother. "I need to talk with Mr. French, please, Jennifer. Put him on the line."

Jennifer held the phone out. "He wants to talk with you."

Howard shook his head rapidly, his eyes huge. "No! No way. I'm not talking to them. Uh-uh." He waved the rifle at her and she had to swallow a gasp. "You talk to 'em."

She slowly brought the phone back to her ear. "He doesn't want to speak with you."

"Okay, okay. That's all right for now, but eventually, I'll need to talk to him. If he changes his mind and wants to speak to me, all you have to do is pick up the phone. It's been reprogrammed to ring me automatically. Understand?"

His voice was so reassuring and confident Jennifer

felt her shoulders ease just a tad. Here was help, she thought. She added a pair of warm brown eyes to the image of the officer she'd made in her mind. "Y-yes. I—I understand," she answered.

"Good. Now answer my questions and don't say anything else. We don't want to upset him any more than he already is. How many people are there, including you and Howard French? Does he have a weapon? Is anyone hurt? Where are the kids?"

Jennifer glanced at the terrified students, then spoke. "Fifteen. Yes. No. At the back of the room."

"All right." She could hear him writing something down, a pen scratching on paper, then the sound stopped. "I'm going to ask you some more questions but first, no matter what happens, keep those kids where they are, okay? We have to know they're in the same location and staying there. Understand?"

"Yes."

"Okay. Now, does he have a gun?"

"Yes."

"A rifle or pistol?"

"The first." She licked her suddenly dry lips. "A .22."

A second passed, as if he were surprised by her recognition of the weapon. She found herself wishing she didn't know.

"Is he calm?"

"For the moment."

"Scared?"

"Yes."

"Violent?"

"No, absolutely not." She dropped her voice. "Howard isn't like that at all. You don't understand. Something must have happened to upset him. Something really bad—"

"Yes, ma'am, something bad happened. He's come into your classroom, taken hostages and has a weapon." He didn't give her time to reply. "Our first priority is you and those children, though. We want everyone in there to come out alive and that's our main goal. We want Mr. French to stay cool. We've got nothing but time, okay? But I've got to talk to him. That's paramount. I can't do my job if I can't talk to him."

"Well, I'm sure he'll talk to you as soon as—"

The moment Jennifer spoke, Howard's eyes flew open and his whole body stiffened. With a practiced movement, he brought the rifle to his shoulder and looked through the sight. "Put down the phone!" he screamed. "Put it down right now or I'll shoot!"

CHAPTER TWO

"JENNIFER! Jennifer... Shit!"

Beck slammed down the phone and wiped his brow. The Winnebago's air-conditioning was cranked all the way up but it didn't seem to matter. The ever present humidity, a damp and sticky gift from the nearby Gulf of Mexico, still managed to creep through the sealed windows. He watched an errant breeze kick up a small cloud of dirt at the center of the deserted playground and cursed again. A month later and there wouldn't have been any kids or teachers in that classroom. "I lost 'em."

"Move him to the end of the classroom. I can set a shot if she gets him by the window."

Randy Tamirisa's voice sounded inside Beck's head, coming through the tiny earpiece he wore. The whole team communicated with each other via a complicated system of earphones and wraparound microphones. As Randy spoke, Lena raised her hand to her ear and Beck knew she'd heard the sniper as well.

"It's way too early—"

"Not yet, Randy—"

Lena and Beck spoke at the same time, but Lena

immediately hushed him with a hand motion and answered the sniper herself.

"Randy, we're not ready for that yet. Stay cool, all right?"

"There're kids in that room."

Beck bit his tongue.

"I know that," Lena said patiently, "but *I'll* let *you* know when it's time to set the shot, not the other way around."

Silence filled their earphones and Beck knew that was all the answer she'd get from her rebuke. He spoke anyway, pulling his microphone closer as if he and Randy were the only ones hearing the conversation. "I haven't even talked to the suspect yet, Tamirisa. I need to establish communications before you get trigger-happy."

Again, Randy didn't answer.

"I need an acknowledgment, Officer." Beck's voice was icy.

Nothing but an absence of sound, then finally— "Ten-four, *Officer.*"

A pointed stick of pain stabbed Beck between his eyes. He resisted the urge to lift his hand and massage the bridge of his nose. The tension headaches were getting worse with each situation.

Showing no outward sign of discomfort, he picked up the phone with an unhurried movement and redialed the number.

Jennifer Barclay answered after the fifteenth ring.

She spoke before Beck could. "He won't talk to you, okay? The only reason he let me answer is because I promised I wouldn't make him talk."

She sounded remarkably collected, and Beck suspected that was for the children's benefit. She didn't want them more scared than they already were, but deep down she had to be terrified. Every hostage was. When someone had total control over your life…you were terrified.

"I understand," Beck answered. "I can work with that. Like I told you before, we've got all the time in the world. There's no hurry. We can wait him out, but ask him this…will he at least listen to me? He doesn't have to answer, okay?"

"Let me see."

Beck heard her put the question to Howard French, then a moment later, she spoke into the phone. "He said he'll listen, but that's all."

"Great. Let me talk with him."

Harsh breathing sounded in Beck's ear. "Howard? I can call you Howard, can't I?"

Silence.

"Listen, Howard, you doing okay in there? Everybody all right? You need anything?" This time, without waiting for an answer, he continued. "I want to help you, Howard. I'm here just for you, but you have to tell us what you want, buddy. We can help you out with almost anything. There's one rule, though, okay?"

Beck's fingers cramped on the phone and he consciously loosened them. ''Are you with me?''

Silence.

''You can't hurt any of those kids. That's the rule. You can't hurt them or the teacher or the school board lady, okay? Once you understand that, we can talk and I can help you out, but you have to tell me you understand me.''

A rustling sound came over the line, then Jennifer Barclay spoke again. ''He said to tell you he won't harm anyone. And I believe him. You won't hurt him, will you?''

Beck looked out the window. It was still light, but the sky had begun to fade into purple, the shadows growing long and dark. He filled his voice with hearty reassurance. ''He'll be fine and so will you and the kids. No one's going to get hurt. Our goal is to keep everyone alive, including Mr. French. I promise you that.''

''He said I could ask for some sodas. He's thirsty....''

''I'd be happy to bring that in. Tell him to send out one of the kids and we'll send in cans of anything he wants.''

He heard another muffled conversation. ''Okay... okay...he says that's fine.'' She spoke once more, but this time in a whisper. ''Look, this guy isn't some kind of wild killer, okay? He's a little simple, but he's not going to shoot anyone. He loves the kids and he loved his job and he's just upset because he got fired. Let me work on him a little bit, okay? I think I can talk to him.''

Beck closed his eyes. *Everyone was an expert.* ''Miss Barclay—Jennifer—the man has a gun. He's assaulted your boss and taken hostages. I understand that you know him and think of him as a friend, but he's dangerous. You need to let us handle this.''

''He *isn't* dangerous,'' she insisted. ''He can't even read, for pity's sake. I've been working with him for months. He's confused and upset, all right? I'm telling you—''

He interrupted her gently. ''Ma'am, we've got a situation here you're unfamiliar with…but we aren't. It's our business so let us take care of it.''

''And just how are you going to accomplish that if he won't talk to you?''

Beck waited a second, then spoke. ''We don't negotiate everything, Miss Barclay. Believe me, we have alternative ways of resolving issues.''

WHEN SHE WAS TEN, Jennifer's father had taken all of them to Disney World for a rare family outing. She didn't want to ride the monster roller coaster, but the cruel gibing she would have gotten from William Barclay had she refused would have been worse. She hadn't known the word then, but *sadistic* came to mean a lot to her as an adult.

She'd looked askance at Danny, but he'd slid his

eyes away from hers and stared off into the distance. He knew how frightened she was, but what choice did she have? What choice had *any* of them had? Afterward, when she'd jumped off the ride, her rubbery legs had given out and she'd collapsed. It was one of the few times she'd failed in front of her father, but it'd given her a taste of what Danny got every day. Her father had never let her forget the incident.

Her legs felt the same way now.

She walked slowly to the rear of the classroom. Howard's eyes were on her back, and she prayed she wouldn't fall down. The children surrounded her as she reached them and kneeled down.

"I want you all to stay back here," she said in a low, reassuring voice, "and don't say anything. I know you're scared, but so is Mr. French." She glanced at Betty—no help there—then again forced her eyes to the children's faces. "He lost his job last week and he doesn't understand what's going on."

"Who called?"

She looked over at Juan and by the quiet way he spoke, she was sure he knew the answer to his question. "It was the police," she said. "They're outside and they're going to help everybody, including Mr. French. But you guys have to do your part and don't move from here. If you need something, Mrs. Whitmire will help you."

Betty nodded but stayed silent.

Jennifer cleared her throat. "Mr. French has asked

the police for some colas and they're going to send some in to us...." She faltered here, not knowing what to do. Which one to send? Which ones to keep? Her gaze fell to Taylor and the answer became clear. The little girl was diabetic; she had to go. Jennifer reached for her. "But...someone has to go get the drinks, so Taylor here is going to help us out."

She put her hand on the child's shoulder and squeezed, leading her to the front of the room. She didn't explain that the little girl wouldn't be coming back. "You'll be fine," Jennifer whispered. "Don't worry." A moment later, Taylor was gone. Howard locked the door behind her, her tennis shoes slapping as she ran down the hallway.

Jennifer listened to the sound with Beck Winters's words ringing in her mind. *We have alternative ways of resolving issues.* She'd seen enough movies to know what he meant. SWAT teams stormed buildings. People got shot. Hostages were killed. Then she remembered what else he'd said. *No one's going to get hurt...I promise you that.*

She didn't know him, of course, but she believed him. Unlike her father, he had the voice of a man who would tell the truth, no matter what.

Jennifer turned back to Howard. One way or the other, she had to try. "What's wrong, Howard? Why are you doing this?"

He lifted his dejected gaze to hers. "I lost my job."

"I know. Remember, I tried to help but—"

"They came and took my truck." His expression was dead and lifeless. "How can I get another job without no truck? How can I pay my rent if I don't have a job?" He started shaking his head before she could even speak. "I ain't going back to that shelter place. There's bad people living there."

Jennifer didn't want to be naive; this man had done just what the cop had said—he'd come into her classroom with a gun and taken hostages—but this was Howard, for God's sake. He was a lost soul. Like Danny.

"You're jumping to conclusions, Howard. Thinking the worst possible thing. Remember how we talked about that when you left here? I told you a positive attitude would help you get another position, remember?"

"And you lied." His voice was blunt. "I went ever'where and I had a real positive attitude, but wouldn't nobody hire me. Said they didn't need nobody." He took a ragged breath and stared out the window. The light drifting through was faint and dim. "That's why I came up here," he said. "I wanted to make Miz Whitmire give me my old job."

Jennifer didn't reply but he shook his head as if she had, his hand tightening on the gun at this side. "When she saw me in the hall, she acted all crazy and ever'thing, and started talking trash to me like she always does. Then she saw my gun, and she tried to run off. She crashed into the door and hit her head. That's how she got the bump. I didn't hit her.''

"Of course you didn't," she said soothingly.

"I—I reached out to help her up and something went off in my head, like an explosion or something. I grabbed her...then I didn't know what to do with her. That's when I saw I was by your door. I knowed you'd help me.''

"And I will, but Howard...what on earth were you doing here with a gun anyway?''

His eyes narrowed. "I was gonna scare 'er. That's all. Just to make her gimme the job back.''

"Well, that plan didn't work too well, did it?" She paused, but he didn't answer. "Let the children go, Howard. Let them go and we'll think up a new plan.''

He didn't appear to even notice she'd said anything. He raised his hand to his bottom lip and pulled gently, then after a minute, he spoke. "That policeman fellow on the phone—he said he'd help me. Do you think he could make her give me my job again? And make 'em give me my truck, too?''

Her heart fell. He simply didn't grasp the seriousness of what he'd done. "I don't know, Howard.''

He stood up and gripped the rifle's barrel with both hands. "You call 'em," he said, nodding his head to the phone. "Tell 'em what I want. You can do it.''

BECK GRABBED THE PHONE even before the first ring ended. "Winters.''

"This is Jennifer. Did Taylor make it out okay?"

"She's fine, just fine. Her mother is here and they're together. I've got the drinks coming. They'll leave it at the door."

"Are the other parents there?"

Beck glanced down the street. Behind a cordon of officers, the media was gathering, along with the gawkers events like this somehow always attracted. Mixed in the throng, there were worried school officials and moms and dads going crazy. Lena had been down twice to reassure them.

"A few of them, yes," he said. Switching gears, he spoke again. "Let me talk to Howard, Jennifer. That's the only way this is going to get resolved."

"He wants me to ask you something," she said, by way of answering. "He wants to know if you can help him get his old job back."

"Tell him anything's possible," Beck said instantly, "but not until I talk to him. I can't help him if I can't talk to him."

Jennifer's voice was soft as she relayed his message. A second later, she spoke again. "He wants his truck, too," she said. "It was repossessed yesterday. He said if you bring his truck to him, he'll talk to you."

"I'll get the truck and we'll talk. But I want another child, too."

She was starting to sound tense, and just around the edges, a little unraveled. Beck glanced at the countdown clock he'd started when he'd gotten there. They'd been at it almost two hours already. It seemed like he'd just arrived; it seemed like he'd been born there. Catching his eye, beside the clock, were the photos Sarah had obtained. With the phone propped against his shoulder, he shuffled through the mess of papers until he came to the one he wanted. The school picture of Jennifer Barclay.

Sometimes when he watched television, he placed bets with himself. He'd close his eyes, switch channels, and listen to whoever was on the screen. Nine times out of ten, he could guess what they looked like by the way they spoke. He would have lost the farm on this one, though. Jennifer Barclay did not match her voice at all. Her chestnut shoulder-length hair was straight and shiny and her gaze was dark and sad. Except for those eyes, she looked much younger than he would have expected. He'd imagined a woman in her forties, someone with a lot of experience behind her, a person who knew and understood others well.

Flipping through the profiles of the suspect and all the hostages Sarah had gotten along with the photos, Beck found the notes on Jennifer. She lived in Fort Walton Beach, in a small condo complex a few blocks off the beach. She drove a white 1995 Toyota Camry, had no outstanding tickets or warrants and she lived alone.

She'd sounded middle-aged, but Jennifer Barclay was young, pretty and single.

She came back on the line. "Okay, he'll do it. As soon as he sees the truck, he'll send another child out."

The line went dead and Beck grabbed the microphone attached to the headset he wore. "Lena? Did you get all that? You got a line on the truck?"

"We're trying. Sarah knew he'd had a vehicle repossessed so she's contacting the dealership now, but they're closed. It's going to take a while."

Beck nodded, but before he could reply, his ear phone crackled to life.

"Get him to the window to see the damned truck. I want to set my shot."

Beck spoke instantly. "That's premature—"

Lena's voice interrupted. "Beck, we don't have another option. We can't do a chemical assault here, not with those kids, and this guy isn't going to surrender. He's not the type and you know it. We need to be prepared just in case." She spoke to someone nearby, then came back over the headset. "While you were talking to the teacher, I told Randy you'd move the guy."

"This is ridiculous." Beck felt his jaw clench, the pain in his head intensifying, his voice going cold. "What are you doing? Trying to make the ten o'clock news?"

When Lena answered, her tone was as chilly as Beck's. "I don't make command decisions based on the media. If you don't know that by now, you should. You're out of line.''

Beck closed his eyes and shook his head. Dammit, what in the hell was he thinking? What in the hell was he *doing?* His head throbbed, and suddenly he felt like the situation was sand slipping through his fingers. Lena had seen what he hadn't in forcing him into taking that vacation. He did need some time off.

But not yet.

"You're right. That was out of line, and I'm sorry," he said stiffly. "But I still think Jennifer's got a point. Howard French doesn't have a sheet and I can get him out of there. Randy should be our last resort, and *you* know *that.*"

"What I know is he didn't have a record before, but not now. Cal called in while you were talking. There's been a new development. It's not good."

"What is it?"

"One of the guys found someone in the mainte-nance shack, out behind the school. We're not sure yet, but it looks like it might be French's supervisor." She took a breath, then spoke. "He's been shot with a .22 rifle."

CHAPTER THREE

BECK'S GUT TIGHTENED. "Damn! Is he dead?"

"He's hanging on but barely."

"Has anyone talked to him?"

"No. He was completely out of it and fading fast. The medics were struggling just to get him to Central before it was too late."

His gaze went to the school, his mind going with it to the woman and children inside. Did Jennifer Barclay know? He answered his own question. Obviously not. She wouldn't be defending Howard French if she knew he'd shot his boss. Would she?

"Get him to the window." Randy spoke bluntly. "It's at the front, away from the kids. If he's looking for the truck, I can get a clean shot."

"And that's it? The decision's made?"

Lena answered. "We're setting the shot, Beck, that's all. I haven't given Randy the green light."

"All right." Beck's words were clipped. "But I think this is premature. I think you're making a mistake, both of you."

"I have to think of the team, Beck. The guys are getting tired and that means they're going to get

sloppy and let their guard down. I can't risk a breakout, either. If he starts shooting…''

''I know the drill, Lena, but those kids in there are
nine and ten years old. Do you want them living with
the sight of a man's brains getting blown out for the
rest of their lives?''

''I want them *to* live, Beck. That's my only concern and it ought to be yours, too.''

''But—''

''If you have a problem with this, we'll discuss it
later.'' She interrupted him, ending the argument
sharply. ''Right now, act like a team member and do
your job. Get the man to the window. When the time
comes, *I'll* decide if we shoot or not.''

THE CHILDREN were getting restless.

Jennifer had done her best to keep them corralled—
without much help from Betty—but they couldn't be
expected to huddle in one corner forever. Howard had
let them use the bathroom attached to the classroom,
but other than that, they hadn't really moved. She
glanced down at her watch and was shocked to see
the time. It was past eight!

The drinks had helped. A dozen cans had been left
outside the classroom. Howard had made Juan re-
trieve them, then report back to him. Were there police in the hallway? No? Was he sure?

It was hot, too, and that *didn't* help. The air-
conditioning had shut down hours ago. It was on an

automatic timer, but Jennifer suspected it'd been purposely shut down early. She pushed a sticky strand of hair off her forehead and glanced toward Howard. He was standing by the door. Obviously growing weary, his expression was one of pure dejection, his shoulders slumped, his face shadowed. The gun had never left his side, and she'd given up the idea of grabbing it. It was just too risky.

They'd talked on and off, but he'd refused to say much more than "It's too late." When she'd pressed him, he'd simply shaken his head, and she'd finally moved to the rear of the room to be near the children. Trying to reassure them, she'd sat down and waited for the phone to ring again.

When it did, though, what would happen? They weren't really going to give Howard his truck…or get his job back for him. He wasn't going to just drive away from the school and off into the sunset. Surely, he understood that.

The phone sounded shrilly, startling her even though she'd expected it. Jennifer looked at Howard and he gave her an almost perceptible nod. She jumped up and ran to the front of the room to grab the receiver. "Hello?"

He answered as he did each time he'd called. "Everyone okay in there?"

Jennifer closed her eyes briefly and leaned against the wall. "We're all right," she said. "But getting tired."

"I understand. It's a tough situation, but you're doing a terrific job keeping everyone together." His voice turned lighter. "How 'bout coming to work for us when this is over? I could get you a negotiator's job. Sound good?"

Jennifer shuddered. "No, thank you. That's way more excitement than I want. Ever."

"It's not all that thrilling. Mainly I sit here, then I talk but no one really listens, and when it's finally settled, I do paperwork. The next day, we do it all over again."

"Sounds like my job."

He chuckled. "Yeah, I guess it does at that. You like being a teacher?"

"I love it," she answered, surprised by his question. It seemed like a strange time to be talking like this, but it made sense in a weird kind of way. He was trying to keep her relaxed. "The kids are fantastic and I feel as if I'm doing something worthwhile. Most days, that is."

"You are doing something worthwhile—all the time—but especially right now. You're holding this thing together, Jennifer, and you really are doing a great job."

For just a second, she almost felt she was somewhere else, in a different time and place. The warmth of his praise eased her fear. "Thanks."

His raspy voice went serious. "So now…you have

to help me some more. The truck's finally on the way. Put Howard on the phone so I can tell him.''

''I'll try.''

Jennifer turned and looked in Howard's direction. He was staring into the distance, his mind obviously not in the present. ''Howard?'' she asked gently. ''Howard? Please come talk to the officer.''

He didn't respond at all. She rested the phone's receiver on a shelf and walked to where he stood. Her stomach in knots, she ignored her fright and spoke firmly, as if talking to one of the children. ''Howard, you need to come talk to Officer Winters. He's on the phone and he has something to tell you.''

''You tell me.''

''No. You need to hear this yourself.''

To her total surprise, he nodded once, then lumbered across the room and picked up the phone. She hurried behind him. He held the receiver to his ear but didn't say anything.

A moment later, he turned and handed her the phone.

Jennifer spoke. ''Yes?''

''I told him the truck's on the way. In the meantime, you're going to have to do something else, too.''

''What?''

Instead of answering, he waited a moment, the seconds ticking by almost audibly. Once again, Jennifer found herself imaging the man behind the voice. His words carried the same timbre of authority her father's always had—academies taught you how to do that, she suspected, military or police, it made no difference—but absent from Beck Winters's tones was the overlay of cruelty her father's voice had always possessed. Winters had children of his own, she decided, and was a good father. Patient. Kind. Loving. Emotions and actions that had been empty words to her father. With a start, she realized she was connecting with Beck Winters, this stranger, on a level she seldom did with men.

"You have to get him to stand by the window. I won't bring the truck down the street until that point."

She felt a flicker of unease. "Why?"

"Because that's how we do things. These are negotiations, and he gets nothing for free. When he sees the truck, then he has to talk to me and release another child. You've got to get him to do this."

Her mouth went dry. "I understand but…"

Beck's voice dropped, and she felt as if he were standing right beside her, his warm eyes on hers. "Jennifer…how else can he see the truck? This is the only way."

Her chest eased a tad and she took a deep breath. He was right, of course.

"It's going to be fine, Jennifer. He trusts you, and I know you can get him to that window. Once he's there, then…then we'll start to talk and I can influence him." He fell silent. "I *have* to be able to talk directly to this guy, Jennifer. The most dangerous hostage takers are the ones who won't talk to me. If I can't get some kind of conversation going with him, this is going to end badly. I can almost guarantee that, especially with Howard's history.''

''His history? What do you mean? He's never done anything like this before.''

The officer answered quickly. ''He's male, he's urban, he has below average intelligence. These are people who turn to violence as an answer. It's not the boss at the steel plant, it's not the manager at the oil company. It's the worker, Jennifer. The poor slob at the bottom who has no control over his life.'' He paused. ''He has nothing to lose. He thinks it's hopeless anyway.''

''I understand how you could read it that way, but you don't know him the way I do—''

''And you don't know everything *I* know.'' He bit off the words, as if he'd said more than he'd planned. ''Just help me out, okay? Are the kids still at the back of the room?''

''Yes.''

''It's imperative you keep them back there. I'll bring the truck down the street as soon as I see Howard at the window. You just get him over there.''

''Okay.''

She started to hang up, but before she could put the receiver down, she heard his voice say her name. She brought the phone back to her ear. ''Yes?''

Static rippled over the line, faint and barely discernable. The noise made her wonder if they were being recorded. "Be careful, Jennifer. Just…be careful."

She started to answer, then realized he was gone. Hanging up the phone, she looked over at Howard and said a silent prayer.

BECK WIPED HIS FACE and looked over at Lena. "Is the truck here yet?"

"There's a traffic tie-up on Highway 98. One Q-Tip rammed another. Surprise, surprise. The road's blocked in both directions, but Dispatch said they'd have it moving in just a few minutes. It should get here anytime."

Beck shook his head. Everyone on the force called the older local residents "Q-Tips" because they all had white hair and wore tennis shoes to match. Florida had its share of elderly drivers, but Beck wasn't sure they were any worse than the tourists who drank too much then got on the road. At least the older people drove slowly.

Lena ducked her head toward the building. "How are they doing? The teacher holding up?"

"She's the only reason there hasn't been gunfire yet. She's keeping French appeased and the kids quiet."

He stared out the window of the motor home into the dusk. They'd cut the electricity to the school and the building had fallen into darkness as soon as the summer sun had dipped behind them, rimming the school in gold. Occasionally he saw the beam of a flashlight near the rear of the room. Beck wasn't surprised to see the teacher was prepared. Classrooms were supposed to have emergency supplies in case of hurricanes, but people forgot, and batteries went bad. Not in Miss Barclay's class, though. He'd bet money she had the correct number of bandages and aspirin as well.

Lena sank into a chair by his side, her fingers going to the shuffle of papers beside the phone. She picked out Jennifer's photo, studying it intently. Without looking at him, she spoke. "She's pretty."

"I hadn't noticed."

Lena's head came up. "Right."

He flicked his eyes toward the picture, but immediately returned his gaze to the school. He didn't need the fuzzy image anymore—Jennifer's face was planted firmly in his brain. Too firmly, in fact. It'd be a while before he was able to get those brown eyes out of his mind, no matter how this all ended. They sat without talking for a few minutes, then Lena spoke once more. "Did you tell her to get him to the window?"

"Yeah."

"What'd she say?"

He turned and looked at her. "I didn't explain why—"

"Of course not."

He turned back. "She'll do it."

Lena leaned forward and put her hand on his arm.

"Beck, listen. I know you don't agree, but we can't let this go on forever—"

Lena had taken off her headset and had been using a radio. It came to life with garbled speech. She pushed the button on the side and barked, "What is it?"

"The truck's here." Lincoln Hood, one of the entry men, spoke, the noise of the crowd behind him filtering into the radio's microphone along with his voice. "I'm switching places with the driver right now, then I'll bring it down the street when you're ready."

"Go slow, Linc," Tamirisa said immediately. "Less than five miles an hour, okay?"

"No problem."

Beck resisted looking at Lena. She stood and paced the tiny aisle. "Listen, Randy—French is going to be facing the window, looking down the street. Are you sure it's going to be a cold shot? If it isn't, I don't want you taking it. Not with those kids in there."

When he'd been younger and gung ho, the euphemisms had meant something to Beck. They'd made him feel as if he were part of a secret club that ordinary cops didn't belong to; now the words made him feel tired and old. Why didn't she just say what she meant?

Can you kill the guy with one shot?

"It'll be so cold, *you'll* freeze." Randy's cocky answer spilled into the room with arrogance. "Hear that, *Officer* Winters?"

"That's enough. I'm not giving you the green light

yet,'' she snapped. ''The man's promised Beck he'll talk so let's see how it goes down first.'' She turned and motioned for Beck to pick up the phone. ''Beck's calling now to get him in place. On my word, Linc, you go. If necessary, *if necessary,* I'll give you the code, Randy, otherwise, standard ops are in effect. Heads up, everyone. This is it.''

JENNIFER JUMPED when the phone rang. She grabbed the receiver. ''Yes?''

''Everyone okay?''

''We're fine.''

''Then it's time. We've got the truck and we're bringing it down the street. You need to get Howard to the window.''

Although it was just as calm and reassuring as always, his voice sounded different. The tension was getting to him, too, Jennifer thought. How could he do this day after day? What kind of man would want this crazy life?

''All right,'' she said. ''We're going right now—''

''Not you!'' Beck's voice went up, then he spoke again, in a more reasonable tone. ''That's not necessary. Use this time to calm the children. Go back to where they are and wait there.''

The suggestion seemed perfectly reasonable.

''Okay,'' she answered.

''Let me talk to him first.''

Holding the receiver at her side, she turned to Howard. He was standing right beside her, the rifle cradled in his arms, crossed before his chest. "They want you at the window, Howard. Your truck is here. But Officer Winters needs to talk to you first."

"No." He shook his head. "Not going," he mumbled. "Won't talk."

"Howard…" She put a warning in her voice, and the students at the back of the room lifted their heads as one. They knew that tone. "You asked for your truck," she said. "And it's here now. You have to be reasonable about this, or Officer Winters isn't going to help you." She held the receiver out to him. "Talk to him. He wants to help you."

"No."

She found patience from somewhere deep inside her. "Why not?"

"Don't want to."

"All right, then. Forget talking to him. Just go to the window and look out. Right now. No more messing around."

He glanced at her, but there was no other warning.

He simply grabbed her and she screamed without thinking. From the back of the room, one of the children cried out. Jennifer dropped the phone. Then Howard dragged her roughly toward the window.

"OH, SHIT!"

"Jennifer!"

"What's going on?" Beck spoke again, overriding Randy's curse. "Randy? Can you see them?"

"He's heading to the window, but…I'm not sure… wait, wait a minute…he's coming to the window. Goddammit—''

Beck leapt from his desk and peered out into the night. It was completely dark now and the outline of the window was nothing more than a square of blackness. He fumbled for the night vision binoculars that had been sitting on the desk but Lena had already grabbed them and brought them to her eyes. "Tamirisa? What's going on? Can you see?''

"He's coming to the window and he's got the teacher with him. Oh, man…I don't frigging believe this!''

"What? What is it?''

"A kid…a little boy…he's just run up to both of them—'' His voice turned deep. "Don't do it, you son of a bitch, don't do it—'' Randy's voice broke off abruptly.

Beck yanked the binoculars out of Lena's hands but before he could even focus, the horrible sound of glass shattering split the humid night air. A second later, a scream followed, the kind of scream he knew would be replayed in his dreams for months to come. When it stopped, Beck heard nothing beyond the beating of his heart.

Another second passed, then that stopped, too.

CHAPTER FOUR

JENNIFER HAD ALWAYS heard time slowed in a moment of crisis.

Not true.

One minute she was standing beside the window, Howard's hand painfully gripping her arm, and the next instant Juan's sturdy ten-year-old frame was flying through the air to knock her unexpectedly to the ground. In less time than could be counted, the two of them pitched to the linoleum, a shower of breaking glass somehow accompanying their fall. Jennifer could think of only one thing: the child in her arms. She had to protect him.

The impact between the hard floor and her shoulder sent pain streaking up her arm then down her spine, but she barely felt it. She forced it away so she could deal with everything else. Raining glass, screaming children, a strange *pop* she couldn't identify at all.

Jennifer lifted her head and stared at Howard. He was standing, exactly where they'd been a second before, but something wasn't right. A small red circle had appeared at the base of his throat. Above this spot, their gazes collided violently then he began to sway. A second later, his mouth became a silent O of surprised betrayal. The rest of his face simply collapsed—a balloon with the air suddenly released. He fell to the floor beside them, and as he landed with a heavy, dull thud, the back of his head disappeared in an exploding red mist.

Jennifer screamed and covered Juan's face with both her hands, but the movement was useless. The child had seen it just as she had—the moment of Howard's death.

She told herself to move, to get up, to do *something* but the odor of cordite hung in the air, sharp and biting, pinning her down. She wanted to gag, but she couldn't do that, either. She couldn't do anything. *He'd promised,* was all she could think. *He'd promised no one would be hurt....*

Juan's urgent voice, crying out in Spanish from somewhere beneath her, finally jarred her. "Señorita Barclay? *¿Qué pasa? ¿Cómo está usted?* Are you okay?"

She rolled off the child and he jumped up, his shocked gaze going instantly to Howard. He covered his mouth with his hand and pointed toward the man, still clutching his rifle. "*¡M-madre de Dios!*"

Jennifer scrambled to her feet. Maybe he wasn't really dead. Maybe it wasn't too late. Maybe she could do something.... Before she could think of what, the door to the classroom opened with a loud bang. Adrenaline surged and she grabbed Juan again.

Shoving him behind her red-flecked skirt, she faced the door.

Men spilled into the room. They were dressed in black, a barrage of noise and brutal action coming with them as they surged inside. They divided by some prearranged, silent signal; one group fanned across the classroom, obviously searching for more danger. Their guns held out before them, they quickly covered every corner and empty space. A second, smaller group raced toward Jennifer and Juan while a third team rushed to the back where the children were screaming.

"Are you all right? You weren't hit, were you? The kids okay?"

A black-garbed figure paused at Jennifer's feet, putting a hand on Howard's neck. Only when she spoke, quickly but with composure, did Jennifer realize the officer was a woman. "W-we're fine," Jennifer answered.

Standing up, the woman nodded then pulled Juan from behind Jennifer and pushed him toward a man waiting behind her. Holding Howard's rifle, he quickly turned away from the body to lead Juan to the back of the room.

"I-is he?"

Though lean and muscular, the woman in black had soft gray eyes and a sweet face. She looked out of place, especially when she said calmly, "He's dead."

A thick fog descended over Jennifer, blanketing all

her emotions but two. Disbelief and betrayal. "He's dead," she repeated numbly.

The woman nodded again, then barked an order to the men surrounding them. To Jennifer, what she said didn't even register but it was obviously an all-clear sign. The words passed through the group like a wave, and in its wake, another figure pushed to the front.

In a daze, Jennifer stared as the man approached. Everything was over—the damage had been done— why now, she thought almost trancelike. Why did time stop now?

He was huge, well over six feet, his chest a blur of black as he moved, his legs so long they covered the distance between the door and the window in three strides. Adults always looked bigger in the classroom where everything was reduced in scale, but this man absolutely towered over the child-size desks and bookcases. Reaching Jennifer's side, he ripped off a black helmet to reveal thick blond hair. It was plastered to his scalp, but the pale strands gleamed, and she realized—illogically at that moment—that the lights were back on. He was intimidating and all at once, she understood the true definition of *authority*. It was none of this, however, that made her feel the clock had stopped.

His eyes did that.

In the fluorescent glare overhead, his cold blue stare leapt out at her. She might have thought the color unnatural, it was so disturbing, but she knew immediately it wasn't. No one in their right mind would actually buy contacts that shade. The color was too unnerving, too strange.

His eerie gaze swept over her bloody clothing then came to a stop on her face. She forced herself into stillness and looked directly at him. When he spoke her name, she recognized his voice.

She knew without asking that this was Beck Winters.

SHE WAS COVERED in blood and bits and pieces of something else Beck noted but didn't need to analyze. For one inane moment, he wanted to pull her into his arms and tell her everything was going to be all right, but he'd be lying if he did. It wouldn't be all right. Not for a very long time—if ever. Not for her, not for the kids, certainly not for Howard French. For the survivors, a hostage incident didn't end when the team busted in.

In fact, Jennifer Barclay's wide brown eyes told him shock had inched its way in, leeching the color from her face and forcing into her eyes the kind of glazed disbelief he'd seen too many times. She'd been stronger than most, but that was over.

It was a mistake of monumental proportions and he knew it, but Beck decided he didn't care. He reached out for her.

She stepped back so quickly she almost slipped and

fell. Grabbing the windowsill behind her, her eyes blazing, she spoke from between gritted teeth. "You bastard!"

Immediately Beck's mask fell into place. Her words weren't what he'd expected, but different people reacted in different ways. He'd once rescued a woman who'd slapped him as he'd carried her out under fire. Jennifer Barclay's anger was a coping technique. She'd been holding her emotions in check for hours and now she was going to erupt.

At him.

Beck took a step away from her and held up his hands, palms out. "Calm down, Miss Barclay, please.... It's over now. You're safe—"

She blinked, and he saw some measure of relief in her expression, something that seemed to loosen for a moment, but she put the response behind her so fast, he almost missed it. Her voice was low but scathing as she lashed out at him. "You lied to me! You promised—*promised*—no one would be hurt." She flicked her eyes downward to where Howard lay. "He's dead!"

"You don't understand—"

"You're damned right I don't understand!" She pushed a strand of hair away from her eyes. They were red and rimmed with exhaustion, her face contorted with the obvious anguish she was feeling. "He wouldn't have killed anyone—"

"He raised his gun at that child."

"He wasn't going to shoot! He was trying to stop Juan from grabbing the gun—"

"That's not how it looked to us."

"But he wouldn't have shot! He wouldn't have done that."

"How can you be sure?"

"I know him, that's how!" Her gaze filled with angry tears. "My God, I told him to go that window and then you shot him! What happened? I can't believe this…."

Beck watched the emotions cross her face. She made no attempt to hide them, but it wouldn't have mattered if she had. He understood better than she did what she was feeling.

I feel guilty because I couldn't stop this.

I feel guilty because I survived.

I feel guilty because I helped.

Before he could say more, Lena broke in. Introducing herself formally, she put her hand on Jennifer's arm and spoke gently. "Miss Barclay, why don't you come with me now? We'll get you cleaned up, then we need to talk to you. Everyone in the room will have to speak to an officer and give their version of what happened."

Jennifer turned her back to Beck and answered Lena quickly, her voice filled with dismay. "Of course…but not the kids—"

She wanted to protect them above all, Beck realized. That was the only thing that mattered to her.

"I'm afraid they'll have to. It's standard, but it's necessary, too. Especially after a shooting."

"My God, I don't believe this…. My students…"

"I know, I know." Lena's attitude was sympathetic and calm. "I've already spoken to Mrs. Whitmire. Our information officer called Dr. Church, the school counselor, and she arrived some time ago. She's with the kids right now, and so is our department psychologist, Dr. Worley. You should talk to the doctors, too. Not just tonight but in the coming days as well."

Jennifer Barclay's full lips were drawn in a narrow line across the bottom of her face. Beck could see traces of pale-pink lipstick she'd put on earlier that day. When her life had been normal. "I don't need to do that."

"You will."

Her gaze shot to Beck as he spoke. Her look was controlled and measured. "What makes you think I'll need help?"

"No one goes through something like this without needing to talk about it later. If you don't, you'll pay for it in ways you can't even imagine."

"I don't have to imagine anything, Mr. Winters." She held out her hands, palms forward, mimicking his earlier action. The smooth skin was sticky with blood and her fingers trembled even as she spoke. "Thanks to you, I've gone through the real thing. I think I'll be able to handle the instant replays on my own."

IT WAS AFTER midnight when they finished. The questions had been endless, and Jennifer had described the situation so many times, she almost felt as if she were telling a story. A story that had happened to someone else, not her. Dr. Church had counseled every one of children and had tried to talk to Jennifer, too. She'd nodded and told the woman she'd call, but she wouldn't. There'd been a police psychologist, too. Another "professional."

Pointless. Simply pointless.

Jennifer would go home, take a hot bath and get into bed. That's what would help her, not talking with some half-baked psychologist. Maybe she'd call Wanda, too. If the other woman had heard what happened—and who wouldn't?—she'd be worried sick.

The press had been satisfied with Betty Whitmire's histrionics and thankfully had left thirty minutes before. Jennifer trudged through the now dark and empty parking lot to her car. She was glad she didn't have to face the cameras and microphones because she didn't think she could. Nothing seemed real to her. How could it? One man she'd known was dead and another was wounded. A second wash of shock came over as she recalled Lieutenant McKinney's words during the debriefing.

"Mr. French said nothing to you about shooting Robert Dalmart? Nothing at all?"

"No. I—I had no idea...."

It must have been an accident. Howard wouldn't

have shot down Robert like some kind of animal. The police lieutenant had told Jennifer that Robert would probably survive, but he'd been injured badly.

The rush of a passing truck caught her attention and Jennifer glanced up in time to catch the white oval of the driver's face. Where was he going? How could he pass by so casually? Didn't he know lives had just been ruined?

She knew she was being ridiculous, but she didn't care. Howard French had been shot before her very eyes. A man who had reminded her of her brother. A man who had trusted her. A man she only wanted to help, but had led to his death instead.

In the back of her mind, a silent voice countered her words. *He'd promised no one would be hurt.*

She reached her car and pulled out her keys but they wouldn't go into the lock. Something was wrong. She struggled with them for a moment, then her hand began to shake and she dropped the ring, somewhere underneath the car door. It was the final straw. She laid her head against the roof of the vehicle and began to cry.

"Can I help?"

Jennifer turned at once. The body armor was gone, but its absence didn't diminish Beck Winters's size. In fact, he looked even taller and more commanding, looming over her car and staring down at her with his stránge, cold eyes. A ripple of anger went through her, but she was too exhausted to even acknowledge it.

"I—I dropped my keys," she said stupidly.

He knelt down, patted the ground beside her feet, then stood. She held out her hand, but he reached past her and slipped the key in. The sound of the door unlocking was unnaturally loud.

"Thank you," she said.

"You're welcome."

There was nothing else to say, but neither of them moved. After a moment, he broke the silence. "Look, I know it's hard to understand what happened back there and I sympathize because this man was your friend, but the team has to save lives—first and foremost. Surely you understand that."

"I told Lieutenant McKinney what I understood," she said. "I don't think you and I need to go over it again."

"Of course," he said stiffly. "I just thought…"

The medic had checked Jennifer and pronounced her all right, but she wondered briefly if he hadn't missed an unseen injury. A painful stab flared in her chest as the cop before her spoke.

"No, you didn't think," she snapped back. "That's the problem with men like you. You put on your uniforms and grab your guns and run out the door to fight. The people left behind are the ones who have to pick up the pieces, but you never consider them!"

As soon as the words were out her mouth, Jennifer

regretted them. They weren't fair and she knew it—they came from a place deep in her past that had nothing to do with the man standing before her—but she was beyond caring. She was completely drained and empty of all logic and reason. She opened her mouth to say so but he stopped her.

"You're right," he said. "But you're wrong, too. The ones left behind do have to pick up the pieces, but I *always* think about them. Believe me, Miss Barclay, they're the reason I do what I do. Seeing someone killed in a situation like this is the *last* thing I want."

He was telling the truth; she could see it in those strange, clear eyes.

"Then what happened in there tonight?" Her voice cracked. "Why was Howard shot?"

"He raised the gun and we thought he was going to shoot the boy," he said raggedly. "Having a sniper in place is standard operating procedure and when he perceived imminent danger to the child, he took the shot."

Something in his voice alerted her. She jerked her head up and stared into the blue ice of his gaze, her stomach churning with the gut feeling that came from hearing the truth mixed with a lie. She wasn't getting the whole story.

She shook her head slowly and stared at him. "I don't believe you. I want the truth. Something went wrong, didn't it? *You* didn't want him killed, did you?''

"Let me take you home," he said gently. "I can call a uniform and catch a ride back up here to get my car. You're in no shape to drive to Fort Walton."

"I'm a teacher, Officer Winters. Diversions don't work with me."

"I'm not trying to divert you. I'm trying to help you. You're wrung out, and you need to get home and take care of yourself."

"So I won't bother you anymore with my questions?"

"No." He paused and took a breath. Was he stalling as he searched for a more satisfying explanation or simply exhausted as she was? "So you won't torture yourself with what-ifs," he said finally. "You did everything you could back there and we did, too. It was a bad end, yes, but it wasn't our fault...or yours."

"He didn't need to be killed," she said stubbornly.

He shocked her by his answer. "Maybe, but we'll never know for sure. Only one thing's certain. We can't go back and play it a different way. We have to take what happened and deal with it."

"Then just tell me the truth. Tell me what really happened—what *I* did—then let me deal with *that*."

From beneath his matted hair, he stared at her, his eyes almost glowing. For a second she caught a fleeting glimpse of something in their cold depths, but she wasn't sure. She was so tired she was imagining it. She had to be.

"I'm sorry." He shook his head, his expression closing against itself. "But I can't tell you more. You'll have to be satisfied with that."

THE MESSAGE LIGHT on her answering machine was blinking furiously when Jennifer finally reached her condo. She hit the play button and closed her eyes.

"I heard about the shooting, and I'm real worried. You call me as soon as you get in. I don't care what time it is, you just call."

Wanda's Southern accent filled the small living room. Normally Jennifer would have picked up the phone and called immediately, but she couldn't make her fingers reach for the receiver. They were as tired as the rest of her, and what little energy she had left, she wanted to use getting clean. She peeled off her clothing, right there in the middle of the den, and walked into the kitchen. Retrieving a paper sack from the pantry, she dropped everything in it and rolled the edges tightly together. Tomorrow she'd burn them.

Naked and shivering in the air-conditioning, she opened the refrigerator. The strongest drink she could find was a bottle of Coors left over from a pizza party some time back. She grabbed it, opened the bottle, and downed the beer. She didn't lower the bottle until it was empty, then she stumbled into her bathroom and opened the shower door. When she stepped out twenty minutes later, her skin was red and raw—whether from the heat of the steaming water or the scrubbing she didn't know.

Her stomach in knots, she knew the only way she could get to sleep was to eat something first. Somewhere between scrambling the eggs and getting the grape jelly out of the refrigerator, she began to cry. The tears ran down her cheeks, but she just ignored them. They weren't going to stop and there was nothing she could do about it so she let them come.

God, how had it happened? One minute she'd been standing beside Howard and the next she'd ordered him to go to that window. No wonder he'd grabbed her—she'd scared him half to death. Then Beck had finished him off.

And she'd trusted him!

He'd sounded so sympathetic over the phone, so caring and warm. In reality, he reminded her of a photograph she'd seen in a sixth-grade world history textbook of a Nordic trapper. He had the same cold, blond looks and size, plus a face like a stony mask. All that was missing were the dogs and sled.

The ringing phone startled her out of her thoughts and her heart thudded in answer against her chest. It took a second for her to regain her composure. Would she ever hear a phone sound again and not jump? Wanda's worried voice could be heard on the answering machine, her drawl even thicker than usual.

"Are you there, girl? What's going on—"

"I'm here, Wanda." Clutching her robe, Jennifer grabbed the phone. "I just got in. I—I'm fine."

"Praise the Lord! I've been worried sick. I heard about what happened at the school, and…well, good grief, honey, are you okay?"

That was all it took. Jennifer began to sob again and several minutes filled with Wanda's "That's okay, now, darlin'" and "C'mon, sugar" passed before her tears subsided. When she hiccuped to a stop, she explained what had happened.

"Oh, my God!" Wanda's concern echoed over the line. She didn't know him but she'd listened to Jennifer's Howard stories time and time again. "And they killed him?"

"Y-yes. Right in front of us. It was terrible, Wanda. I—I can't believe it actually happened. And I helped!"

"But, honey, he might have murdered every one of y'all."

"Wanda! You've heard me talk about him! Do you really think he would have shot us?"

"He shot that poor other man."

"It must have been an accident! Howard wouldn't have just walked up and done it in cold blood. He wasn't like that."

"But you said he raised the gun when Juan ran over."

"He did but he was trying to keep it away from Juan. When he saw Howard dragging me to the window, Juan thought I was in danger. He ran over to grab the gun.''

"Are you sure? Absolutely positive?"

In the background, Jennifer could hear canned laughter coming from Wanda's television. She lived alone and when she was home, it was on.

"How do you know Howard was just keepin' that gun away from the boy?" Wanda continued, cutting off Jennifer's potential answer. "He could have been bringin' it up to shoot. You don't know! You just don't know."

"No." Jennifer replied immediately. "I'm sure he wasn't—"

"Why? What makes you so sure? Haven't you ever been wrong before, Jennifer? I certainly have and I can't imagine that you haven't been in all your thirty-six years."

Despite her Southern ways, Wanda never minced words. Jennifer swallowed, her throat tight. "I have been wrong before, certainly."

"We never know what's in another person's mind, sugar." The nurse's voice softened. "We just don't know. You could be mistaken. Howard French was a strange duck. He coulda been liftin' that rifle to shoot that poor little boy. You better think long and hard before you set what you think in stone."

They talked a few more minutes after that, Wanda reassuring Jennifer her mother was fine. "We turned off the TV so she wouldn't hear all the news. She seemed pretty foggy today, but you never know what's soakin' in and what isn't.''

"Thanks for watching out for her."

"Oh, honey, you're welcome. You just don't worry about her. I know you won't listen to me, but you take care of yourself...and if you wanna talk some more, you call me, hear?''

Walking to the balcony off her living room a few minutes later, Jennifer stood and looked at the sky. There was no moon and only the twinkling lights from a few houses here and there alleviated the dark. She wasn't close enough to the beach to hear the ocean, but if she leaned all the way to the left at one end of the narrow patio, she could catch a glimpse of the water. She did so now, but all she saw was blackness.

We never know what's in another person's mind.

Wanda was right. You couldn't tell for sure what someone else was thinking, but some things you just knew. And Jennifer knew—for sure—that Howard French would never have shot Juan Canales in cold blood. She just knew.

Beck Winters had made a terrible mistake.

And she'd helped him.

"Go ahead," her father taunted. *"Do it. Do it."*

Holding her breath, her ten-year-old lungs about to burst, Jennifer watched in horror as Danny peered up at the twenty-five-foot pole. Her brother's fingers tightened on the rope, and his eyes grew even larger.

"You aren't man enough to do it, are you?" William Barclay's voice was as sharp as his words, cruel and unforgiving. "You can't do anything right. You can't even climb a pole! Hell, kid, your scrawny little sister can make it up that damned stick. Why the hell can't you? You can't do anything but mess around with that damn paintbrush of yours!"

Jennifer opened her mouth to cry out, but her warning was trapped, somewhere deep inside her. She managed to make some kind of sound, and her brother glanced in her direction. That's when his face changed into Howard's.

Jennifer tried to scream, but still no sound came. She lifted her fingers to her mouth and understood why. Her lips were sewn shut.

Horrified, she jerked her head in her father's direction, knowing without asking, he'd been the one to make her silent. But her father wasn't there anymore. Betty Whitmire stood where he'd been.

"It doesn't take a brain surgeon!" she cried. "Just mop the floors, French. Mop the floors!" Standing at Betty's side was Dr. Church and another woman. She didn't immediately recognize her, but Jennifer knew who she was anyway. Dr. Worley, the police psychologist. As Jennifer watched, they turned, very slowly and deliberately, until their backs were to what was happening.

Jennifer whipped her head around to where Howard stood. The rope had changed into a mop, but as she watched, Howard lifted it and fired. The bullet came out in slow motion and finally, when it hit the target, Jennifer was able to scream.

Betty had turned into Danny. "Help me," he cried, clutching his chest. "Help me, Jennifer! You're the only one who can...."

Gasping for breath, she called out Danny's name then she woke up, choking. For one terrifying second a stabbing pain burned in her own chest. Clenching her nightgown with both hands, she rose up on her knees, tangling herself in the covers she'd been fighting, swaying and almost falling. Then suddenly it was over. Her mind took control of her body, and she gasped, cold, sweet air rushing painfully into her lungs.

Covered in sweat, Jennifer collapsed on the bed and began to cry.

CHAPTER FIVE

THE CEMETERY was ringed with oleanders. Their emerald branches swayed in the Saturday morning breeze as Beck leaned against his car and waited for Jennifer. Howard French's autopsy had been cursory, the funeral scheduled quickly. In the crowd surrounding the grave site, Beck spotted Jennifer easily. Her chestnut hair had a mind of its own; strands had already escaped the knot at the back of her head and they too, were moving in the wind.

He crossed his arms and told himself he had no business being there, waiting for her. Just like he'd had no business talking to her in the school parking lot after the incident. It wasn't against the rules, but getting involved with victims was never a good idea. He needed a certain perspective on every case and growing close to someone involved made that task hard.

This situation was even tougher though, because Jennifer Barclay wanted more answers than he could give. Like most civilians, she didn't understand he couldn't tell her more. He couldn't tell her he hadn't wanted Randy to shoot. And he couldn't tell her about the fight they'd had afterward. The team was just that—a team—and both he and Randy had to keep their mouths shut. Lena had promised Beck an informal investigation and he felt damned lucky to get that. It meant she'd pull him and Randy into a room and grill them until she dressed down either one or both of them severely. But the results would never be public.

Regardless of all that, he'd come to Lawndale at 10:00 a.m. on the dot, knowing Jennifer Barclay would be there, and knowing, too, he wanted to see her, just one more time. He didn't understand why the need was so strong, but it was there, and he couldn't ignore it. Something about her was different, and he wanted to figure it out. Figure *her* out.

He waited patiently and half an hour later, the mourners around the casket began to move away. There was no limousine to carry off grieving family members. French had had no family.

Jennifer picked her way across the lush green grass. She was wearing a dark-navy dress and was having a hard time walking, because her heels were sinking into the lawn. She seemed smaller than he remembered, less self-assured. Maybe because she wasn't surrounded by the authority her classroom gave her.

A woman walked with her, talking as they moved through the headstones. Dressed as somberly as Jennifer, she had an expression of concern on her face and glanced at Jennifer with almost every step they took. She was trying to convince Jennifer of something; Beck could read body language as easily as he could listen to and understand a conversation and he wondered what she wanted. As they came closer to Beck, she put her hand on Jennifer's arm and pulled her to a stop.

He strained to catch their words. One or two floated toward him on the wind.

"...come stay with me..."

"...absolutely not..."

"...can't sleep, can't eat..."

Obviously disagreeing, Jennifer shook her head vehemently at the woman, and that's when she saw Beck. Her body stiffened and the graceful arch of her back went ramrod straight. Their gazes met across the verdant lawn, the marble angels watching to see what would happen next.

Beck wondered as well. She looked as if she wanted to run the other way, to escape as fast as she could but he was leaning against *her* car. If she wanted to go home, she had to come to where he stood.

She said something to her companion and the other woman turned her head in Beck's direction. She scrutinized him, then nodded once. She didn't smile, but he felt no animosity in her frank appraisal, only curiosity and something he couldn't quite interpret. She hugged Jennifer tightly, rubbing circles on her back before releasing her to walk away. Beck hadn't a clue who she was, but she clearly cared a great deal about Jennifer.

When she got to the car, he could see Jennifer had been crying. Her brown eyes were teary and a bit of mascara was smeared beneath her thick lower lashes on the right side.

Without thinking, he reached out and rubbed his thumb on the spot. She blinked in surprise but otherwise stood still.

"Mascara," he explained.

She lifted her hand and with the back of one slim finger touched the same place he had. "I don't know why I bother. It inevitably ends up where it shouldn't."

"My ex-wife always blamed me for that," he said gruffly.

"Did you make her cry?"

She wasn't going to make it easy for him. Beck nodded slowly. "Sometimes."

As if thinking about his answer, she stared past him to watch the line of cars disappear, then she faced him once more. He could see now, in the ribbons of sun streaming through the trees, that her eyes were more than sad. They were filled with exhaustion, deep shadows ringing them with the puffy look that came from not sleeping. She appeared thinner, too. He'd assumed it was the dress, but all at once he wasn't sure.

"Why are you here, Officer Winters?" she asked. "What are you doing?"

"It's Beck," he said. "My first name is Beck."

She didn't reply so he reached into his shirt pocket and removed a business card. He held it out to her, but she took so long to accept it he thought for a minute she was going to refuse. Finally her fingers curled around the card, brushing his hand with a softness he wanted to ignore.

If she recognized the name, she gave no indication. After reading the card she looked up at him. "Dr. Maria Worley?"

"She's our police psychologist, the one who came after the incident. I want her to visit your classroom next week along with me. I know it's almost the end of the school year, but I don't think those kids should leave without seeing her at least one more time."

"Dr. Church already mentioned this to me." She tried to hand back the card but he kept his arms crossed. She fingered the square a bit more, then gave up and stuffed it into the pocket of her dress. "She's very competent. She doesn't need assistance."

"I agree, but we spoke and she decided that Dr. Worley might help. She specializes in this kind of trauma. Dr. Church felt a little overwhelmed, especially since she knew Howard, too."

Her voice revealed her skepticism, but she nodded wearily. "Well, if that's what Dr. Church wants…"

"It is. Betty Whitmire thinks it would be a good idea, too."

Jennifer's expression shifted instantly. "Betty Whitmire wouldn't know a good idea if it bit her on the butt. She's incompetent, tactless and part of the reason all this happened. She shouldn't have fired Howard. He was a good worker."

Her candor surprised him and he chuckled. "Don't like your boss?"

"I hold her responsible. Just as I do you."

His amusement evaporated under the heat of her words. "That's fine," he said evenly. "I'm accountable for my actions."

"Including Howard's death?"

"I didn't pull the trigger. That's not how it works."

"Then tell me how it *does* work." Her eyes flared, the conversation taking on an animosity he hadn't anticipated but should have. "Tell me how I managed to get Howard to that window—for you—and then he was killed. Tell me how you aren't responsible for that."

"I can't."

"You can't what? Tell me the truth or be held accountable?"

"Either."

"But you lied to me."

"And I would again," he said harshly. "That's what I do for a living, Jennifer. I lie to people to make them do what I want them to. So I can save lives."

Disgust and frustration fought their way across her once smooth brow, but before she could say anything more, the roar of a backhoe stopped her. She turned to look and he followed her gaze. The workers had lowered the metal casket and were covering it with dirt.

The sight clearly drained her anger. She faced him once more.

"But there's more to it than just that, isn't there? And you won't tell me the rest, will you?"

Beck felt a tug at the boundaries that divided his work from his emotions. Dixie, his ex-wife, had never asked…because she'd never cared. This was different, though. Jennifer cared almost more than she should.

He kept the struggle from his voice. "You were there, Jennifer. You don't need my interpretation. You *saw* what happened."

She made a low, rueful sound. "And Wanda says I can't even trust that."

"Wanda?"

She nodded behind her. "The woman who was with me. Wanda LaFleur. She's my mother's nurse. And my best friend."

"Your mother's sick?"

"She's at Seacrest. She has Alzheimer's."

"I'm sorry to hear that."

Jennifer nodded but said nothing. The cemetery was only a few blocks from the beach, and the seagulls soared overhead, their raucous calls breaking the silence between them. Now Beck understood what he'd seen earlier. Jennifer and Wanda LaFleur were friends, but Wanda was a nurse as well, and she was trying to get Jennifer to take care of herself. She wasn't sleeping well or eating right. The thought coalesced in his mind with everything else he'd learned, and all at once, with crystalline clarity he understood who Jennifer Barclay was.

She put everyone else first and if there was anything left, then she gave it to herself.

She wouldn't seek help on her own. People like her didn't. He had to try anyway.

"You need to talk to Dr. Worley, along with your students. She's an excellent listener and she'll understand what you're going through. She understands post-traumatic stress."

Jennifer's dark eyes flashed. "I appreciate your concern, but I'm not 'going through' anything, including post-traumatic stress."

"No nightmares or insomnia? No depression? Howard French was your friend. You might have experienced some of those things even if you hadn't seen him shot."

She regarded him silently, with an iciness he might have worn himself. He bore the chilly stare better than most, probably because he knew the pain it could hide.

"The doc's a good shrink," he said finally.

"Is that the voice of experience?"

He gave her a level look. He could cloak his feelings, too. "Would it make any difference if it was?"

"I don't know." Her expression thawed slightly. "I'm sorry, I didn't mean to pry. I—I'm upset, that's all." She waved her hand toward the grave. "The funeral and everything…"

"It's okay," he answered. "I'm being pushy, too." He stopped because he didn't know what else to say. How could he tell her what he really thought? *I think you're beautiful and intriguing, and I don't want to see you hurt more than you already are?*

"I'm simply trying to help," he said. "That's all."

"And I appreciate it," she answered stiffly. "But I don't need your assistance. I've been taking care of myself for a long time. I can handle this, too."

JENNIFER DROVE to the nursing home with her windows down. It was sweltering outside and the dark linen dress she'd worn to the funeral felt sticky and limp. Underneath the sleeveless shift, however, a coldness had seeped into her body and refused to leave. She didn't know whether she should shiver or wipe her brow.

Beck Winters left her feeling that way.

Had he saved lives or simply ended Howard's?

She'd almost fainted when she'd seen him leaning on her car. For the past few days, she'd thought about him a lot. In the middle of a math lesson, his image would pop into her mind. While reading aloud to the class, she'd suddenly recall his eyes. She knew these interruptions were just her brain's way of dealing with everything that had happened: It was far easier to think of Beck Winters than it was to remember the blood. But she had to wonder why her psyche had picked him, of all people. It couldn't be because she was interested in him. Absolutely not.

She hadn't dated anyone seriously since Andy McCall. She desperately wanted to be married and to have a family of her own, and he'd seemed like the perfect choice. A fellow teacher, Andy had been the kind of man she'd always wanted, or so she thought: stable, responsible, totally unlike her father. When he'd proposed, though, she'd turned him down. Something important was missing from their relationship. Something vital, even though she couldn't name it.

She pulled into the driveway of the nursing home and parked. The breeze was slightly cooler here— closer to the bay—but the emotional riot going on in her head didn't take note. In fact, she felt even warmer as her thoughts returned without permission to the man who'd waited for her at the cemetery.

She hadn't thought it possible, but his eyes had looked even bluer in the daylight, almost electric. And in their depths, she'd seen a hint of something that piqued her interest. It wasn't sympathy. After her brother's death, she'd developed a finely tuned radar for that emotion. No, this was something else and she wasn't sure what. Reaching into her pocket she pulled out the card he'd given her and laid it on the dash.

Dr. Maria Worley Psychologist. The address was for a commercial building near the center of town, close to the bridge that spanned Highway 98 as it crossed from Destin to Fort Walton.

Jennifer stared at the business card a moment longer, then she grabbed her purse and got out of the car, leaving the card to curl in the humid heat. No matter what had been in Beck's eyes, she wasn't going to a therapist to deal with Howard's death. She knew firsthand they simply did no good.

A few minutes later, Jennifer entered the glass doors of the nursing home. Walking briskly to the brightly painted wing that housed the ambulatory patients, she nodded to the security gaurd and several of the nurses as she passed. Her mother had been in Seacrest for five years and Jennifer knew everyone. The facility was always spotless and the staff really cared about their patients. They didn't just line the halls with wheelchairs; they planned activities and even gave certain patients small tasks like feeding Smoky, the home's fat gray Persian.

When Jennifer entered her mother's room, she found it empty.

Her heart skipped a beat, and she hurried over to the nurses' station in search of Wanda.

One of the aides saw Jennifer and smiled. ''Your

mom's outside," she said, tilting her head toward the patio just beyond the window. "It's such a nice morning, we thought she might enjoy the breeze. She's having a very good day."

Jennifer's pulse slowed. "And Wanda?"

"She's with a doctor. I'll tell her you're here."

Jennifer murmured her thanks then turned to go through the nearby double doors. She stopped at the last minute and looked at her mother through the glass.

She was sitting in a glider, her profile sharp and lean, her silver hair pulled back and coiled in one of Wanda's elaborate French braids. She wore a double-knit pantsuit with flared legs and an elastic waist. She refused to wear anything else, and Jennifer had to haunt secondhand shops to even find them for her. She often wondered if Nadine liked them because she'd worn them in the seventies, before Danny's death—when things had been perfect, if only in Nadine's mind. She looked healthy and was physically fit but her mind never seemed to be in the present. Sometimes she was thirty and Danny was a little boy, Jennifer not even born yet. Other days, Nadine was older and Jennifer a toddler. The days were scarce where her mother lived in a world that had known Danny but lost him.

Jennifer understood completely. For a while, she'd done the very same thing.

Pushing through the doors, she crossed the patio

and came to where her mother sat. "Hi, Mom," she said. "How are you?"

Nadine Barclay looked up at her daughter and smiled sweetly. "Oh, you look so pretty! Are you a new nurse?"

With a sigh, Jennifer sat down in a nearby chair. "No, Mom, it's me, remember? Jennifer. I'm your daughter."

It hurt each time she had to remind her mother of who she was, but what else could she do?

"Jennifer?" Nadine said uncertainly.

"That's right." Jennifer nodded. "Your daughter."

"Jennifer..." She brightened suddenly. "Have you seen Danny? How is he?"

They went through this on Nadine's good days. When she understood who Jennifer was, she always asked about Danny. At first, Jennifer had wondered why Nadine never asked about her, but over time, the painful torture had ceased to matter. There were too many other things to worry about.

"He's fine, Mom," Jennifer answered automatically. "He's gonna come see you next week."

"Oh, good!"

Nadine smiled with satisfaction and pushed the glider back into motion, saying nothing else. A lot of times their visits went this way. After greeting each other, they'd sit for half an hour in silence, each lost in thought, then Jennifer would rouse herself and leave, feeling vaguely guilty that she hadn't tried to engage her mother more. She made a vow today to try harder.

"I saw Mr. Winters again," Jennifer said. "You remember me telling you about him? He was the policeman at school the other day?"

Nadine's eyes rounded briefly. "Policeman? Did he have on a uniform?"

Her mother hated the sight of any man in a uniform. She'd get terribly upset. Wanda had to keep her in her room when the UPS man made his deliveries. It would have been funny if Jennifer hadn't understood the reason her mother felt this way. She not only understood, she shared the feeling. A quick glimpse of a uniformed man, especially in fatigues, and her throat would swell up and she'd be a terrified ten-year-old again—a little girl whose father had been in the Navy Special Ops.

Jennifer wasn't sure her mother would perceive Beck's black T-shirt and pants as a uniform but she avoided answering the question all the same. It was simpler that way. "He's a member of the SWAT team. I told you about him."

"Oh, yes..." Nadine resumed her rocking.

"He gave me a business card, from a psychologist he knows. She works for the police and he wants me to talk to her. He said she could help me."

"That's nice, honey."

Jennifer glanced at her mother. Nadine hadn't understood a word of what she'd said. When Jennifer had told her mother about the hostage incident, she'd looked up to find Nadine sleeping soundly.

"I'm not going," she said, almost to herself. "Those kinds of doctors never do anything, and besides, I'm handling the situation just fine."

"Yeah, sure you are. That's why you aren't sleeping and you look like a scarecrow!"

Jennifer didn't even turn around. "If you're going to join our conversation, the least you can do is sit down."

Wanda's rubber shoes squeaked as she crossed the covered patio and came to Jennifer's side. "That's all I have to say."

Jennifer arched her eyebrows and stared at her friend. She'd changed clothes, replacing her dark dress with pink cotton pants and a bright top. The cheerful colors made her skin look even smoother than it normally did. "Really? That'd be a first!"

They grinned at each other, then Wanda dragged a chair across the tiled floor and plopped down in it. "Well, actually, I do have some more to say—"

"Of course you do."

"Don't go interrupting me. It's important."

"I'm sure it is. Everything you have to say is important."

"Well, you bet it is! Miss Nadine, you know that's so, don't you?"

The older woman smiled vacantly. "Yes, dear, that's true."

Wanda looked at Jennifer. "See there? Your momma knows how smart I am."

Jennifer couldn't help but smile. "Of course she thinks you're smart. Sometimes she thinks I'm Barbara Walters, too."

"That's okay. There's worse people she could accuse you of being." Wanda leaned over and patted Nadine's leg, then turned back to Jennifer. "What I was going to say before I was so rudely interrupted is that Officer Winters is right. Why not visit this psychologist? She might help."

Jennifer rolled her eyes.

"Hey! This is me! Wanda. You've already told me you're not sleeping and it's more than obvious you aren't eating, either. You're skin and bones."

Deep inside, Jennifer heard a begging teenaged voice, which she ignored. "You know my feelings on this, Wanda. My brother saw a therapist for years. What good did it do him?"

"Your brother has nothing to do with this."

Jennifer sighed. "I know, I know, but I can't stop thinking about him. Betty Whitmire talked to Howard just like my dad always did to Danny. *'Why didn't you catch that ball? It was thrown right at you! Your sister would have caught it!'*" In a higher tone, she spoke again. "*'Why can't you clean up this toilet?*

Any fool could see it's still dirty! Do that one again, Mr. French!'"

Wanda just shook her head. "You are going to drive yourself crazy over this, girl. Howard French was a criminal! Your brother died trying to prove something to your jackass of a father. There was no connection. The fact is, this goes way past the doctor, honey."

"What do you mean?"

Wanda's voice turned gentle. "Beck Winters is trying to help you because he likes you."

Jennifer shook her head. Wanda was forever trying to link her to someone; she wanted her married off with babies on the way. Jennifer wanted the same thing, but she wanted to find the right someone first. "You've been tending to your patients too long. I think you're the one losing your mind."

Now it was Wanda's turn to be stubborn. "You are wrong, wrong, wrong."

"Wrong." Nadine repeated. "You're wrong."

"See there! Your momma knows."

"You're both nuts," Jennifer replied. "The man's a total stranger. For God's sake, Wanda, you didn't even meet him. How on earth could you say what you just did?"

"I didn't have to meet him. He waited for you in ninety-degree heat for more than half an hour. For what? To give you a business card? C'mon, girl. Use your brain for something besides those damned kids you're always trying to teach.''

Jennifer blinked, Beck's image swimming before her. "That's his job," she said. "He was just doing his job.''

"No. He was doing his job when he tried to get Howard French out of that classroom.''

"And that's the best reason in the world not to have anything to do with him…even if he was interested,'' she added.

Wanda simply shook her head.

"You don't understand, Wanda. The least he could do is explain what really happened. I'm sure there's more to the situation than I was told about, and I want to know what it was.''

"Why? Do you just want him to admit a mistake was made? He wouldn't do that, even if it was so.''

"I need to know the truth. It's important!''

"Well, if something else went on, that's his business, not yours. He knew what he was doing, Jennifer. It's his job. And he doesn't have to defend it to you.'' Wanda leaned closer. "And I'll say it again. He didn't drive out to that funeral and stand in that heat just to hand you that card. Think about it. You're a smart girl. You can figure out the real reason.''

CHAPTER SIX

WANDA'S implication was stupid. Just plain stupid.

Even if Beck were interested in Jennifer—which he wasn't—and even if he hadn't been involved with Howard's death—which he was—there was no way she'd even remotely consider him. Jennifer wanted a peaceful, calm life. Orderly and planned. Beck obviously lived the exact opposite way. With a job like his, it was inevitable. Always on call, constantly facing chaos and violence. She shuddered, her crazy childhood coming back to her in a flash. Her father always running off in the middle of the night to somewhere strange, none of them knowing where he was. Her mother all upset.

No. Jennifer wanted nothing to do with a man like that.

As she worried over the conversation, a noise sounded behind her. Her heart in her throat, Jennifer whirled around. Beck Winters stood in the doorway.

They stared at each other across the classroom. She'd been expecting him; he was there to talk to the kids, but as she met his gaze, Jennifer felt as if she'd made a terrible mistake in allowing his visit. Could

he read minds? Could he tell what she'd been thinking? She told herself she was being absurd, but the
intensity in his eyes had her wondering. Breaking the
eye contact, Jennifer looked at the woman standing
beside him.

Jennifer vaguely remembered meeting her that
night, but she'd been too shocked to really notice the
police psychologist. Petite and well dressed, Maria
Worley looked to be in her midthirties. She had dark
hair and lively eyes. As she and Beck came closer all
Jennifer could think was she didn't look like a psychologist. That made no sense, of course, therapists
didn't look a certain way, but her open and friendly
manner surprised Jennifer.

They shook hands and made conversation, but moments later the students began to stream into the classroom. Grateful for the ensuing confusion Jennifer
watched the kids tumble in and grab their seats.
Through it all, she could feel Beck's stare like a hand
against her back.

Finally the children sat down and settled in, and
Jennifer began to speak. "We have guests today. Officer Beck Winters and Dr. Maria Worley. As I mentioned before, they're going to talk to us about what
happened with Mr. French and take any questions you
may have."

Jennifer stopped and took a deep breath. She didn't
even know if she was making sense or not she was
so conscious of Beck's presence. It felt as though they

were connected by some invisible bond. She didn't like the feeling, but what could she do? Forcing herself to focus, she said, "I want you to feel free to talk to our visitors about anything, anything at all, okay?"

Her pulse still jumping, she walked to the back of the classroom. Beck rose and began to address the rapt and silent group.

Jennifer could tell what people really thought by the way they talked to her students. If they didn't respect the kids, they talked down to them. If they felt uncomfortable in the classroom, they often did the opposite and talked over their heads. Beck did neither. He struck exactly the right chord when he told them who he was and began to speak. The debriefing they'd gone through right after the incident had helped, but in the time since, the questions and issues had been simmering. She hadn't realized how much until now.

The first question came from Cherise. The little blonde held up her hand in a tentative way, her eyes darting to Jennifer instead of Beck. Jennifer smiled encouragingly as Beck answered the child. "You have a question?"

Jennifer could see her gather herself. "My mom said he was dead, but is he really? Mr. French, I mean?"

Beck nodded, a serious expression on his face, his electric blue eyes thoughtful. "Your mom is right.

Mr. French died. We're very upset that it ended that way, but bad things happen when guns are involved."

Three more hands popped up, and he pointed to Juan. "You first. Go ahead."

Juan spoke softly, but as soon as he did, Jennifer's heart broke. "Are his friends mad?"

Beck frowned. "I'm afraid I don't understand. You mean, Mr. French's friends?"

The little boy nodded. There weren't gangs in Destin as there were in the larger cities, but even still, the kids knew about them. Jennifer started to explain then Beck's expression cleared as he realized what was going on.

"I'm sure Mr. French had friends who are sad he died, but they aren't going to come to the school, I can promise you that. You're safe and it's not going to happen again. He acted alone...." Beck stopped, his gaze searching the children's faces. "Do you understand what I'm saying? I mean he wasn't part of any group. What he did, he did by himself because he was upset and angry. Sometimes people do things like that when they're confused."

Julian put up his hand, speaking at the same time. "But it could happen again, couldn't it? Somebody else could get a gun and come in here and start shooting and everything—"

"They could, but they won't," Beck said firmly. "What happened is a rare thing. Think about it. In all the years that the school has been here, has anything like this happened before?''

The kids all shook their heads and more than one or two seemed to relax and ease back in their chairs. Jennifer stared in amazement; Beck handled them like a pro, and she wouldn't have done half as well herself. By the time he brought Maria to the front of the room, the students were ready to deal with the deeper emotional issues.

As they'd already arranged, Jennifer and Beck slipped out into the hall. The psychologist had told Jennifer she wanted to see the children alone at first, then possibly later with her in the room.

Walking quickly, Jennifer led Beck to one of the courtyards outside. He held the door open for her, and Jennifer brushed past him, catching just a whiff of a spicy aftershave. His chest seemed to be a mile wide, and by the time she reached the bench in the center of the little patio, she was having a hard time breathing.

She sat down, again feeling the strange connection to him, but trying to ignore it. She pretended instead to concentrate on the beauty of the garden. She often came here to calm herself. Each year a different class took over the care and tending of the small plot, and this year's gardeners had obviously been studying vines. In the humid air of the early afternoon, the sweet scent of Carolina jasmine was mixed with honeysuckle. Normally, just smelling the flowers would make her feel better, but today it didn't work its usual magic. The silence felt too heavy, and she had to break it. She spoke nervously.

"You were very good back there," she said, inclining her head toward the building. "You have an excellent feel for what the kids need to hear. Sometimes people tell them too much and other people don't quite know what to say. It gets complicated, I guess, but—" She realized she was babbling and stopped abruptly.

He seemed surprised by her compliment, and for just a second, she could have sworn the blue ice of his eyes thawed.

"I like kids," he said. "They're innocent and I don't see much of that in my work."

She couldn't help herself. She had to ask. "Do you have children of your own?"

"No. My ex-wife didn't want a family and she didn't stick around long enough for me to convince her otherwise. We were only married two years." He lifted his foot and rested it on the bench, draping his arm across his bended knee as he looked at her. "How 'bout you?"

"I've never been married," she said. "But someday, I'd like a family. A big one." She often thought of having a houseful of children and dogs and noise and confusion. What would it be like?

"Do you have lots of brothers and sisters?"

"I had one brother, but he's no longer alive."

"I'm sorry."

"It happened a long time ago." She paused, the remembrance too painful. "A lifetime ago." Searching for a different topic so he wouldn't ask any more questions, she spoke again quickly. "Have you always been a negotiator?"

He looked at her with those strange eyes and she could tell he knew exactly what she was doing. He answered anyway. "No," he said, shaking his head. "I used to be one of the tact group. I was a front entry man."

When she frowned in confusion, he explained. "It's another position on the SWAT team. I'd be the first guy inside when we'd have to do an assault."

She thought of Howard and his rifle. "That sounds dangerous."

"Not any more so than the rest of the positions but it definitely had its bad points." An unreadable expression crossed his face. "I lasted five years, then I had to get out. I was going to quit the team, but Lena wouldn't let me. She sent me back to school for more training and I came out a negotiator."

Jennifer studied his profile, then something clicked and she understood what she was seeing. She encountered the same emotion in the mirror every morning. It was guilt. A warm rush of sympathy came over her, and despite not wanting it at all, she felt the bond between them tighten even more.

"What happened?" she asked softly. "Why'd you want out?"

His mouth, usually full and generous, she realized all at once, narrowed into a slash. "It's not something I talk about," he said coldly.

"I—I'm sorry," she said quickly. "I just thought…"

He straightened his back and stood. "It's a boring story, that's all. You don't really want to hear it." He nodded toward the classroom. "Why don't you tell me why you became a teacher instead? That would be much more interesting."

"I've always loved children." She answered automatically while the rest of her was wondered what he was hiding. Obviously she'd hit a nerve as sensitive to him as Danny's death was to her. "I like helping them learn."

"And why here? Are you from Destin?"

"I'm not from anywhere. My dad was in the navy, and one of his last stops was Hulbert Field. When he came home and said 'We're moving' again, I refused. I was seventeen and we'd lived in twenty different houses. I got a job and an apartment and settled in and finished school. I haven't left since."

"Where is he now? Still traveling?"

"My father died ten years ago from a heart attack, and Mom came back here and bought a house. She'd loved the area as much as I did and had hated to go. She stayed in her home until about five years ago, then when she couldn't really look after herself anymore, I got her a place at Seacrest.''

"You've been on your own for a long time."

She met his gaze. "I was on my own before they moved."

He nodded and started to sit down again, but he froze in midmotion, his hand going to his beeper. Snatching the black box from his belt, he stared at it intently, then raised his head. "I've got to go," he said. "Can you get Dr. Worley a cab when she finishes?"

"Of course." Jennifer jumped to her feet. "But what's going on? Is something wrong?"

He'd already turned and was striding toward the door. "It's a call for the team." As if that explained everything, he said nothing more and a second later he was gone.

Standing alone in the courtyard, Jennifer watched the door swing shut, then a stark memory flooded her; the image of her mother watching her father leave.

"When will you be back?" she'd asked tearfully.

"When it's over," was all he'd said.

Her mother had cried herself to sleep every night until he'd returned. Three months later.

"GOD TOLD HIM TO DO IT."

Beck stared down at the woman before him. She was a tiny thing, no more than five feet tall and no more than forty years old. Her face had the wrinkled appearance of a dried prune, though. There wasn't an inch of skin the sun hadn't aged into a leatherlike surface. She was way too young to look as she did, but the hard, dark tan, and her anxiety, added an extra ten years. Every few minutes she'd jerk her head over her shoulder to stare at her apartment.

"God told him, huh?"

She nodded, her hair flying as she turned back to face Beck. "He talks to God a lot. He's only fifteen but he's very religious. This morning, when he called me at work, he said 'Mother, God told me you're a sinner and I should make you pay. I'm following his orders.'"

Beck glanced back toward the weathered apartment building. It held only four units, each one with an identical door facing the street and a small rectangular window to its left. The bottom half of the windows were blocked with small air conditioners. "Then what happened?"

"I heard him start to trash the place. Glass breakin' everywhere, things a-crashin'. I screamed at him to stop, but it was too late. He'd already ripped the phone out of the wall, I guess. The line went dead. When I got here, he wouldn't let me in and that's when I called the police."

"And what time did he call you, Mrs. Stone?"

"About two or three, I think."

They were standing beside a cruiser in the hot afternoon sun. The War Wagon was parked down the street with Bradley Thompson, the assistant commander, inside, coordinating everything. Beck had come outside to talk to the mother.

"And there are no weapons in the house, right?" He'd already been briefed, but it never hurt to double-check.

"I don't believe in guns. And I'd know if he'd brought one in. I got an eye for that kinda thing."

The woman worried a cheap silver ring with her fingers, twisting it around and around.

Beck spoke gently. "Where's your husband, Mrs. Stone?"

In the bright light, her gaze dropped to the street, then she spoke with defeat. "He's up at Raiford. He won't be home for a while."

Beck knew what she meant without further explanation. Raiford, a small town near Jacksonville, was the home of the Union Correctional Institution. Among others, it housed Florida's Death Row inmates. Obviously Mr. Stone had not been a model citizen. Beck felt a weary stab behind his eyes as he placed his hand on her shoulder and squeezed reassuringly.

"We appreciate your help, Mrs. Stone. Why don't you let Officer Greenberg get you some coffee, and I'll try to talk to your son."

Waiting nearby for Beck's signal, Sarah started forward to lead the woman away. She started to go with the information officer, but she stopped at the rear of the vehicle and squinted back at Beck, a hand above her eyes to shade them. Heat rolled over them in waves. Her voice turned thready as it rode one toward him. "You—you won't hurt 'em, will you? He's just a kid."

"Absolutely not," Beck said automatically. "Our goal is to get him out of there, that's all." He hadn't finished the sentence when Jennifer's face replaced the mother's worried countenance. "It'll be all right," he said and prayed he was telling the truth.

She started to cry as she left, her thin shoulders shaking. Sarah put an arm around her and bent her head to listen as the woman sobbed.

Beck watched them leave, his own head beginning to pound as his cell phone rang. He grabbed it off his belt. "Winters."

"Things okay down there?" Lena sounded almost as anxious the woman who'd just left. She wanted to be at every site and monitor every event, but she'd sent Beck and the Alpha Team with Thompson this time. As the team's specialist in security, she'd taken a dignitary protection assignment at the Civic Center for the state's local senator who was speaking that evening.

"It's fine," Beck answered. "Just an upset kid who's trashing his mother's apartment. The arriving officers didn't think he had any weapons but they couldn't get him to come out so they called us. We can't get him to answer the phone—looks like he destroyed it or the line, so I'm gonna bullhorn him in a minute. If that doesn't work, I'll throw in a cell phone. No weapons, nobody hurt…just a little misunderstanding.''

''Good.'' She sounded relieved. ''Call me back if it heats up. I can be there in five.''

A second later, Beck crossed the street and stood behind the car of the patrol officer who'd first arrived on the scene. It was the closest vehicle and offered the best protection. He lifted the bullhorn to his mouth and spoke, hating it as his voice boomed across the pavement. He preferred to use a phone. ''Stephen? Stephen Stone? Can you hear me? This is Officer Beck Winters.''

Beside Beck stood Lincoln Hood and Edward Ventor, two of the three front entry men. The rear men, Cal and Jason, were already stationed at the back door of the apartment.

The blinds above the air conditioner twitched and the two men at Beck's side tensed, their weapons at the ready. Beck spoke into his headset. ''He's at the window, everyone. Heads up.''

The blinds moved again, separating enough for Beck to see a face. A young, scared face.

He raised the bullhorn to his mouth once more. ''Stephen, I want you to come outside right now with your hands over your head. When you get out here, lie down on the sidewalk. No one will hurt you.

We're here to help, buddy. But you have to come out first."

The blinds dropped back down.

Sarah's voice came over Beck's headset. "I've got the neighbor here, Beck. The woman who lives in the apartment on the right-hand side. If you don't want to risk a direct assault through the back door, then Cal and Jason can go into her unit and break through the connecting wall."

"Can they get in her place without him seeing them?"

"I think so," she answered quickly. "I've got the floor plans to the units. There are no windows in the back, just the door."

"Okay," Beck answered. "Keep the neighbor here and stay cool. I don't think it's that serious yet, but you might have a good plan—"

"Shit, man, look at that!" Beside him Linc Hood pointed to the door. "I think he's coming out."

The front door was covered by a screen, making it hard to see exactly what was going on. With no hesitation, the men beside him lifted their weapons. Beck tensed. "Stephen, if you're coming out, then do it. Come out and lie down. But don't do anything else."

The screen door opened wider and a kid stepped out into the glaring sun. He was skinny, his face scarred by acne, limp dark hair falling over one eye. Sometime during his rampage, he'd hurt himself. There was a cut running down one arm, blood staining the edge of his T-shirt. Hardly a seasoned criminal.

But everyone held their breath as he stood on the sidewalk. You never knew, Beck thought, you just never knew. A second later, the kid dropped to the concrete, face down. Lincoln and Ed immediately ran to the young boy's side. They had him cuffed and dragged to his feet within a few moments, but not before Beck had time to notice the teenager's shoulders jerking and shaking just as his mother's had a few minutes earlier.

He was crying.

Once Beck would have felt the satisfaction of knowing the incident was over and no one had gotten hurt, but all he could think about was how easily it could have ended a much different way.

And then he thought of Jennifer.

Pushing her out of his mind, Beck headed toward the youngster. "You okay?" he asked.

The teen raised his head, but he wouldn't look Beck in the eyes. If Beck had seen him on the street, he wouldn't have thought him twelve, much less fifteen. He looked pitiful and terrified all at the same time, and Beck couldn't help but feel sorry for him.

"I'm all right," he mumbled.

Beck nodded to the two men and they led the boy away. As they reached the patrol car, Mrs. Stone ran up to them and threw her arms around her son.

He watched for a moment, then Beck joined the

knot of men who'd already begun to gather near the War Wagon. After such a simple incident, the debriefing wouldn't take long and in anticipation, some of them were already shedding the heavy, hot Kevlar they were forced to wear. As Beck removed his own vest and helmet, Bradley Thompson separated himself from the group and came up to where Beck stood, extending one beefy hand. The assistant commander of the team had been a military policeman and he still carried himself with the regal bearing most MP's possessed.

"Good job, Beck," he boomed. "Zero casualties and one successful mission! Excellent."

Randy Tamirisa came to where they stood. "Yeah, Officer Winters. Excellent job!" His black eyes narrowed. "You're a real miracle worker getting a fifteen-year-old kid to surrender!"

A few of the men standing nearby chuckled. They didn't hear the undercurrent of challenge in the younger man's voice. They functioned as part of a team and that kind of razzing was expected. Beck knew better, though. Randy wasn't teasing.

But Beck also knew better than to encourage the countersniper. If he said nothing at all, the younger man would get even more frustrated. With an almost perverse pleasure, Beck pointedly ignored him. "Thanks, Bradley," he answered, pumping the man's hand once then dropping it. "It was a good effort on everyone's part."

"Yeah, but kinda boring, wasn't it?" Randy patted the stock of his weapon. "I didn't get to do my part like I did last week. You guys need to try a little less hard."

The rest of the men shifted uneasily. This time Randy's voice held an obviously disrespectful tone.

"That's the goal, Randy," Beck answered coolly. "We don't want to use you any more than we have to. I'd think you feel the same way as a member of this team."

The younger man jutted out his jaw, his black eyes glinting in the hot sunshine. "I don't need you telling me how to feel, Officer Winters. You telling me how to do my job is bad enough."

Beck's pent-up frustration with the younger man got the best of him. "I wouldn't have to if you did it right."

The black-garbed sniper took two steps and thrust himself into Beck's face. "I do my job better than anyone else on this sorry-ass team," he growled. "And I don't appreciate you saying otherwise."

Beck stayed exactly where he was, noting with satisfaction the younger man had to crane his head to look at him and express the empty threat.

"You're full of shit," he said softly. "I'd trade any one of these men for two of you. They have experience and brains—you've got dick."

Just as Beck had known, his words were all it took. Dropping his weapon, the younger man raised a fist and took a wild swing. Beck calmly blocked the blow with the side of his hand. Before Randy could do anything else, Beck folded his fingers over the sniper's fist and squeezed hard. His knuckles cracking, Randy let out an agonized grunt and his eyes narrowed in a squint of pain. He couldn't do anything but go along as Beck dragged him closer and pushed his face into Randy's.

"You're a menace to this team and the civilians who need us." Beck's voice was a cold roll of thunder. "Get a grip on your emotions, or I'll see that you're out of here."

IT WAS Sunday afternoon. Jennifer had gone to church, washed all her laundry, read the paper...and there was nothing else to do. Usually she had her day all mapped out in advance, but as she moved restlessly about the condo, the walls seemed to move in on her, and everything she'd planned seemed pointless and dull. She thought briefly of walking down to the beach, but dismissed the idea. The churning emerald water, rolling in and rolling out, wouldn't work its usual magic and calm her; she knew that without even thinking twice.

Impulsively grabbing her car keys, she stabbed her feet into a pair of sandals and headed out the door, not even bothering to change clothes. For once, her shorts would just have to serve. Twenty minutes later, she was pulling into the parking lot at Seacrest.

The Sunday staff was smaller. Wanda, one of the senior nurses, never worked that day. Not quite knowing why she was there herself, Jennifer went inside the nursing home and made her way to her mother's room. She opened the door slowly. It was a little past two and she expected just what she saw. Her mother lying in bed.

Jennifer slipped inside and sat down in the plump cushioned chair that rested in one corner. For a long time, she stared at her mother as she slept. Her face looked lovely, the skin smooth and marblelike, her hair spread over the pillow like strands of woven silver. Gradually Jennifer felt the morning's tension ease from her body. She gave in to the feeling, not understanding, but accepting it. After a little while, she began to talk.

"I don't know what to do, Mom," she said, feeling a little foolish, but not letting that stop her. "I saw Beck Winters again on Friday and I don't understand it."

Her mother murmured in her sleep, as if encouraging Jennifer.

"He's not the kind of man I want in my life. Not at all. In fact, as we were talking, his beeper went off and he ran out the door on a call. It reminded me so much of when Daddy used to leave and how you hated that. I asked Beck where he was going and he didn't even answer me.

"But...I keep thinking about him! It's driving me

nuts. I've never been obsessed with a man in my life, but for some stupid reason, I just can't quit thinking of him. He's so tall and well, dammit, he *is* good-looking. I think that's part of it. I've never actually been close to a man that overwhelming.

"And his eyes, my God, those eyes..." Jennifer shuttered her own gaze as she thought about Beck. "I've never seen that shade of blue before. There's something almost hypnotic about it." She glanced at the motionless figure on the bed. "But it's more than just how he looks, Mom. It's a lot more. He was so kind to the children and so considerate. How can one man be two different people?"

Nadine didn't answer, of course, and Jennifer didn't expect her to. Sometimes there weren't answers, she was learning.

Which brought her full circle. The more she thought about it, the more uncertain Jennifer became. What if Beck had been right? What if Howard *had* shot Juan? How would Jennifer be feeling right now if that precious little boy had died?

Jennifer's eyes went back to her mother. As she watched, Nadine raised her hand to her face. Tucking it under her cheek, she turned on her side and started snoring softly. Jennifer stood then stepped next to the bed and bent over to kiss her. She spoke softly. "I love you, Mom."

By the time she got home, she felt strangely better. Not completely calm, but not as anxious as she had been, either. She went out to her balcony then sat down to watch the sun set.

In her mind, Beck Winters sat beside her. She didn't like the image, but it wouldn't go away.

CHAPTER SEVEN

THE PARTY ON Friday night at Betty Whitmire's house had been planned since the beginning of the semester, and she saw no reason to cancel it. "We want to end the school year well," she'd announced pompously. "I'd appreciate a good turnout."

Jennifer didn't need the reminder. Betty might irritate her, but with everything else that had happened, Jennifer was actually looking forward to tonight's event. She needed to get out and mingle. To forget. Every time she went to sleep, her rest was interrupted by the same horrible nightmare. And during the day, she kept thinking of Beck—the man she wasn't interested in.

Worst of all, last week, waiting in line to check out at Delchamps she'd had a flashback to the moment Howard had died. Someone behind her had dropped a jar of mustard. The yellow goo had gone everywhere, but Jennifer hardly noticed. It was the sound that set her off. And for just one second, her lungs quit working. She gasped, catching herself at the very last moment from actually dropping to the floor. The teenager behind the grocery store's register stared at her strangely, but Jennifer simply abandoned her cart and dashed from the store. She didn't care what anyone thought. All she wanted was escape. Careening into the parking lot, she'd thought her heart was going to explode it was pounding so hard.

When she'd climbed into her car, she'd immediately spotted Maria Worley's card and in a fit of frustration, she'd crumpled it up and tossed it out the window.

With a conscious effort, she put the problem behind her and focused on the present. She was going to a party and she wanted to have a good time. Walking up the sidewalk leading to Betty's house, Jennifer felt her white dress wrap itself around her legs, whipping back and forth in the fresh, evening breeze. Betty lived in Sandestin, near the bay, and her home was her pride and joy. Gracious and perfectly maintained, the house was a reflection of the others surrounding it. Sandestin was one of the nicest neighborhoods in the area.

Betty greeted Jennifer at the door, the perfect hostess as always. She smiled and pulled Jennifer inside. "Oh, don't you look darling," she said, her eyes sweeping over Jennifer's haltered sundress. "So casual, too! Just the right touch for a pool party...."

Jennifer didn't need a dictionary to translate. Betty's gold lamé jumpsuit offered the most obvious clue. Jennifer smiled anyway, determined to have a good time. "I'm glad you approve," she replied.

"It's already so hot, I thought this might be the most comfortable."

"And a smart choice it is, young lady!" Betty's husband came into the marbled entry and smiled warmly at Jennifer.

How the two of them managed to stay married, Jennifer had no idea. A well-respected local physician, Waylon Whitmire was one of the kindest men she knew. He held out both his hands then took hers and kissed her on one cheek.

"You look as beautiful as always, my dear," he said. His eyes crinkled and he shook his head. "I was awfully sorry to hear about what happened in your classroom. I hope you're doing all right."

"I'm fine," Jennifer lied, "but thank you for asking. That's very sweet of you."

"Oh, he's not just being concerned, Jennifer!" Betty raised one eyebrow and eyed her sharply. "He's being professional. When you go through what you and I did, you have to be careful, you know. I spoke at length with Dr. Worley and she says we might very well experience PTSD." She leaned closer. "That's Post-Traumatic Stress Disorder. The symptoms include insomnia and depression, or you can have nightmares. You can even have flashbacks—"

"I know what PTSD is, Betty." Jennifer tried to keep her voice polite.

"Well, that's good. Because I've arranged for you to see Dr. Worley. In fact, I've decided to make your interview with her part of your year-end evaluation for this school year. The district will pay for it, of course.''

Jennifer's jaw actually dropped. She could feel it, along with a flood of dismay. ''Are you kidding?''

''Absolutely not,'' Betty replied. ''Dr. Worley understands what we experienced.'' She lowered her voice. ''You have to *deal* with these things, Jennifer. You can't ignore them.''

Jennifer began to sputter. ''I—I don't think talking to a shrink should impact my job evaluation, Betty! Th-that's not fair.''

''Please, Jennifer!'' Betty patted her on the arm. ''Surely you know me too well to think that! I'm not *basing* your evaluation on your little talk with the doctor. Good heavens, I won't even know what the two of you discuss.'' She wiggled her fingers in the direction of her husband. ''Doctor-patient confidentiality, you know. I just want you to have a chat with her, that's all. She's a wonderful listener and it will do you a world of good.''

''But, Betty—''

Ignoring Jennifer's look of dismay, Betty glanced into the mirror hanging at Jennifer's back. When her expression returned to Jennifer's, she smiled vacantly. ''Why don't you run along inside and join everyone and we'll talk about it on Monday. Just have fun this evening.''

Waylon's sympathetic gaze raked Jennifer's face as

Betty clutched his arm and dragged him with her to the door to greet their next guests. Jennifer stared after them for a moment longer, then she turned with a sick feeling in the pit of her stomach. Having fun was the last thing that was going to happen to her now. What on earth did Betty think she was doing? Making her way into the Whitmires' elegant living room, Jennifer shook her head. Betty meddled in everything and that's why she'd run for the school board. She wasn't really malicious, or at least, Jennifer didn't think she was. Clueless was more likely.

Either way it didn't matter. The results were the same.

But there was nothing she could do about it tonight, Jennifer decided. On Monday morning, they could fight over it. Spying Cindy, the teacher whose classroom was opposite hers, Jennifer nodded and headed toward the covered outdoor patio where the other woman stood. Maybe she could salvage something from the evening. If nothing else, they could gossip and drink and eat the delicious hors d'oeuvres Betty always provided.

Jennifer was halfway across the room when she saw him.

Beck stood head and shoulders above everyone else in the crowd, his blond hair shining under the low-level lights. He was completely alone, standing near the bar, with a drink in his hand. And he was watching her.

All at once she turned into a column of wood and became incapable of moving. As if he knew she couldn't escape him, he started slowly toward her, his eyes never leaving hers. She felt like a mouse being stalked by a lion. As he cut through the party-goers, her pulse began to sound loudly in her ears, competing against the chatter of the guests and the music playing somewhere in the back of the house. By the time he reached her side, Jennifer was sure he could hear her thumping heart.

He had on navy slacks and a white shirt, and his hair was slicked back, off his face. "Surprised to see me?"

She had to swallow twice before she could answer him. "I—I— Yes," she finally managed to say. "I am surprised. Betty invited you?"

He nodded. "When I brought Dr. Worley to the school last Friday. She said she wanted to 'reward' us."

"Us? Is the doctor here, too?"

"I'm not sure. But she invited Lena—you remember her?—too." He lifted his drink to the patio outside. "She's around here somewhere. She's got her date in tow."

Jennifer nodded, the gist of the conversation flowing by her unheeded by any attention. "How was your call?" she asked. "The one you had to go to after you spoke to the class?"

"Just fine." His answer was quick and his tone matched it. *Don't ask anymore,* he seemed to say.

She hardened her heart as she looked up at him, but it didn't seem to matter. He still got to her. He was, without a doubt, one of the best-looking men she'd ever met, but there was more to Beck than just that, and finally she realized what it was. He was magnetic. There was no other word for it. She didn't want to like him. She hated what he did and how he lived his life…but she couldn't have walked away from him any more than she could have stopped the sun from shining. Simply standing beside him, she could feel an actual physical pull toward him. She fought it with everything she had in her and even took a step back from him.

"I was on my way to visit with a friend outside. I'll just head that way, I guess…." She let her words die out.

His eyes searched her face as he answered, but at the same time, he stepped to one side. "Of course, I won't keep you." Then their gazes met, and suddenly, once more, Jennifer couldn't move.

For a long moment, they just stared at each other. She might have doubted it before, but she no longer could: Beck felt the unseen cord that linked them, just as she did. Those blue eyes reflected the knowledge back at her. The revelation made her shiver.

"Maybe later we could share a drink?"

She didn't say a word—she couldn't. She just nodded.

"I'll find you," he said.

"Okay…"

She forced movement into her legs, made herself start to walk off, but without any warning, he reached out and put his hand on her arm. His fingers were hot, not just warm, and the heat burned through her bare skin and went straight into her bones. She almost flinched, but the feeling seemed like such a contradiction, she thought she might be imagining it. How could a man who looked so cold and forbidding have such a blistering touch?

He gazed down at her. "Don't try to get away without talking to me, now. I'm a cop…I'll find you."

He was teasing her, she knew, and waiting for a smile or a reaction, but Jennifer could give neither to him. She could do nothing but nod.

And maybe that *was* the reaction, she thought as she crossed the room.

Whatever he asked, Beck left her no answer but yes.

BECK WATCHED Jennifer head toward a set of double doors that opened on to the patio. Just as she reached them, she paused and looked back over her shoulder. He lifted his drink in a silent promise, and she nodded, as though she understood his message. *I'll be waiting.*

It was more than just a promise, he thought, watching her slim, bare back depart. No catastrophe he could imagine would keep him from finding her later. When she'd walked into the room, her white sundress baring tanned arms and legs, her chestnut hair gleaming, he'd been unable to catch his breath, along with every other man in the room, he was sure. He'd thought before that she was pretty, thought she was attractive, but he hadn't seen her like *this*.

She was sexy. Sensual. Incredibly desirable.

He was still staring out to the patio when Lena appeared at his side.

"What are you doing, Winters? Stargazing?"

Beck pulled his attention away from the doors. Lena's right hand was linked with the man standing next to her, her date, Nate Allen. The police chief of Pensacola, Nate nodded briefly at Beck, then stared down at Lena. All the men teased her about Nate's infatuation. He doted on her and she hardly seemed to notice. A few years before, she'd been about to marry, but it hadn't worked out. Every time Beck saw her with someone, he knew her heart was still in the past and it pained him.

"I was talking to Jennifer Barclay," Beck answered.

He waited for a smart-aleck remark, but Lena merely nodded vaguely. "Nice lady. Seems sharp." She appeared distracted, her mind somewhere far beyond Betty Whitmire's living room.

Bending toward her, Nate spoke. "Would you like a drink, sweetheart?"

"Yes," she answered quickly. "A glass of cola would be great."

He nodded then looked at Beck and raised one eyebrow. "May I get you something, too, Beck?" His voice was polite as ever, but underneath the veneer Beck sensed the same tension that was in Lena's eyes. Had Nate asked her to marry him and been turned down again?

Beck raised the bottle of imported beer he'd taken when he arrived. "I'm fine."

Nate nodded curtly, then vanished into the throng. Beck watched him disappear, just as he'd watched Jennifer. Beside him, Lena did the same. For a few seconds, they stood together silently, then Beck noticed what she was doing. She was removing then replacing the tiny gold ring Nate had given her at Christmas. On. Off. On. Off. She wore it on her right hand—it was not an engagement ring—but it looked as though she wouldn't be wearing it at all soon.

"Everything okay?"

She looked up at him in surprise as he spoke. "Of course. Everything's perfect. Why wouldn't it be?"

"I don't know. You just seem a little tense."

"It's fine...*I'm* fine." As though the words were spoken for her own benefit as much as his, she nodded her head in emphasis. "It's going great."

She was trying too hard to convince him, and suddenly she seemed to realize it. Her expression shifted, and she seemed to switch gears. Beck could almost hear them grinding as she went to safer ground.

"I heard you and Randy had a problem," she said. "At the Stone call-out."

"Yes, we did. You should have been there. He's a bomb waiting to go off."

"That's funny. Bradley used just about those same words to describe you to me. He said you almost came to blows."

"Randy was shooting off his mouth. I'm getting tired of it."

"I am, too," she said, surprising him. "He's more hotheaded and impulsive than I'd first thought, but it's my job to worry about the team, not yours."

"He's going to get someone hurt," Beck said darkly.

He could have said more, but he broke off and looked toward the patio doors. Lena's gaze continued to drill his profile. He could feel it.

"You need a vacation," she said, her voice flat. "I want you to go ahead and take off like you were planning to before the Westside situation. Next week."

"I can't."

"Of course you can—"

"I can't." He interrupted bluntly. "I've got a seminar down in Panama City already scheduled. I was going to do it when I came back. I don't have enough time to leave and do that, too. I can't take off now. Maybe later.''

He could still feel her scrutiny, but he refused to look down. Finally, she sighed heavily. ''All right. But I'm not fooling, Beck. You need a vacation. You're getting the thousand-yard stare in your eyes, and I don't like it. I want you out of here in the next month. One way or the other.''

JENNIFER WAS RECLINING in a lounge chair by the edge of the pool when Beck found her an hour later. Partially hidden by the drooping fronds of a huge sago palm, she'd thought—hoped?—he wouldn't spot her, but no such luck. He prowled around the circumference of the turquoise water, until he came to where she sat. The light from the swimming pool bathed their faces with a flickering glow. Beyond the edge of the yard, the darkness of the bay shimmered endlessly.

She looked up at him. ''You're not mixing and mingling?''

He took the lounge chair next to hers and stretched out, the steel-and-mesh frame creaking beneath his weight. His feet, covered in soft leather loafers, hung over the end a good six inches. ''I met everyone,'' he said. ''They seem like nice people....''

She heard the hesitation in his voice, read it and supplied the unspoken ending to his sentence. ''But all they wanted to do was talk about what happened.''

He nodded slowly. "That just about sums it up."

"Not exactly party talk."

He stared into the water, his voice meditative. "You'd think I'd be used to it by now, wouldn't you? When the team gets together, it's always shop talk, but I guess I thought it might be different tonight."

His remarks surprised her. All her father had ever talked about was his work. It had consumed him, and she'd always made the assumption that men who thrived on adrenaline were like that. But Beck *didn't* want to talk about his job?

"They're just interested, that's all, You're someone different," she explained. "We've all worked together for years so when someone new turns up, everyone wants to talk to him. And, well…"

He waited.

"Besides that…"

He laughed as she hesitated again. "What? Don't tell me teachers are cop groupies."

She laughed, too. "Maybe, but frankly, we have a lot of unmarried women at Westside. I'm sure no one missed their chance to check you out."

He shook his head in a rueful gesture. "And here I thought it was my charm and personality they were after."

She smiled back in the darkness and spoke without thinking, something that was beginning to be a habit, she decided. "You *are* charming. I'm sure that had something to do with it."

She immediately felt awkward in the aftermath of the compliment, but it didn't seem to bother Beck. In fact, he shifted in his chair and stared at her. "I didn't think you held that high an opinion of me."

Folding the edge of her skirt between her fingers, she fussed with the fabric as she thought of what to say. It was hard to organize her thoughts. Beck's proximity threw a net of confusion over her that she just couldn't seem to escape. "Maybe I spoke too quickly that day," she said finally. "The day Howard died... All I had was your voice. I was in shock when it was over and—"

"You don't have to explain."

"But I want to," she answered, looking over at him. "I need to. You sounded so kind and caring over the phone. You were a real lifeline for me. That's why I was so shocked when—when it ended as it did. I had imagined you as someone much different."

He sat up and locked his laser beam gaze on hers. "I am the person you heard, Jennifer. I care more than you can possibly understand even if I don't always show it the way you think I should. Don't judge me by what happened that day."

His words were a rumble on the humid air, and for just a second, she almost expected lightning as well. "I don't have anything else to go on," she answered.

"Then let me give you something. Let me show you how I'm different. Get to know me better."

Her stomach flipped over. "I don't think that would be a good idea."

"Why not?"

"I just don't."

He reached out and took her hand in his, and again, the heat was instantaneous. She almost snatched her fingers back, but at the very last moment, managed to resist the impulse. He raised his eyes and met her gaze. "What are you so afraid of?"

She did pull her hand away then. "I'm not afraid of anything," she answered. "I don't think it'd work."

"Tell me what I could do to change that."

"I can't think of anything."

"Do you date at all?"

She flushed. "Of course I date."

"So if I were someone else, you'd say yes? We could go out, maybe have some dinner then get to know each other better and after that we'd decide if we wanted to take it further. But since I'm me, you've made that decision already. Is that it?"

She spoke hotly, feeling trapped. "Do you negotiate everything?"

He laughed then and leaned closer to her, dropping his voice as the darkness wrapped them together more intimately than she would have thought possible. She fought back a shiver.

"This isn't negotiating, Jennifer. When I decide to

do that, you won't even know it's happened until it's over.''

As his blue eyes locked on hers, his implication became clear, and her face flamed even more.

"C'mon," he said. "I promise I won't bite."

He might not bite, but he was still dangerous and she knew it. Men like Beck needed excitement, tension, stress in their lives, and she wanted none of that in hers. She labored hard to keep her existence as ordered and tranquil as she could and getting involved with a man like him would disrupt everything she'd worked for since she'd left her father's house. No matter how intriguing he might be. No matter how hot his touch.

"I'm sorry," she said firmly. "But you'll have to take my word on this. It wouldn't work."

CHAPTER EIGHT

THE FOLLOWING Wednesday, Beck walked out of Maria Worley's office and into sunshine so hot and bright, it momentarily blinded him. He slipped on his sunglasses and glanced at his watch, thinking about the meeting he'd just had. SWAT team members regularly presented lectures to the various nearby police departments. The information helped the other officers with potential problems and kept them all in touch, a good thing if they had to work together to resolve a situation. When his topic involved psychological issues, Beck always spoke with Maria as part of his preparation. The woman was smart, and her recommendations never failed to be helpful.

Ignoring the sweltering late-afternoon heat, Beck stared back at the building. He should have been asking the good doctor for dating advice instead. Jennifer's rejection had stung more than he'd expected. He wasn't the kind of guy who thought women should swoon at his feet, but Beck generally didn't have them refuse his first offer straight out.

He understood her reasons, of course. Jennifer was holding on to a ton of anger. He suspected part of it came from somewhere in her past, and he could do nothing about that. The rest sprung directly from the incident with Howard French. She might not blame Beck anymore, but she had questions and she didn't trust him. He wanted to try to erase that doubt from her mind and assure her everything possible had been done to keep Howard alive. Beck didn't know if he could do that, though.

For one thing, he wasn't so sure he believed it *was* the truth. For another, it didn't matter. It was over and done with, and Beck never looked back. It did no good.

Still, he'd wanted to try and she'd rejected him.

After she'd turned Beck down, Jennifer had explained Betty Whitmire's plans. He'd wanted so badly to pull her into his arms, he'd almost been able to feel her curves beneath his hands, but he'd held back. He told himself now it was possible her rebuff had more to do with that situation than it had to do with him. She was upset, right? How could she think about a date when she was worried about talking to Maria?

"Why don't you want to talk with Dr. Worley?" he'd asked.

Jennifer had crossed her arms and regarded him with dark eyes. "I don't believe in psychologists," she'd answered. "My brother saw one for quite a while before his death, and it didn't help him at all."

The mention of her brother sharpened Beck's attention. He considered asking her once more what had happened, but something told him she wouldn't tell him the details until she was ready. "Maybe he wasn't a good doctor."

Her glare chilled. "That goes without saying."

"Maria's good at her job," he persisted. "In fact, she's excellent."

Jennifer didn't answer. He hesitated, then reluctantly gave in to the silent urging he was hearing in his head. How could he hold back if what he knew might help the woman standing in front of him?

"Do you remember asking me a while back if I'd seen Maria personally?"

"Yes…"

"Well, I have. It's not something I like to recall, but the fact is a few years ago we lost several men during a standoff. Every one of the guys on the team had to go see her. Some of them didn't want to, but Lena made it mandatory, and it turns out she was right to do so. We were all suffering from the same thing. Blocking out what had happened, having flashbacks, feeling angry. Avoiding thinking about the problem altogether." He stopped. There was no way he could explain everything—he didn't even want to—so he kept it simple. "It was bad."

Jennifer's expression shifted slightly. "What happened? How did—how did these guys die?"

"You don't want to know."

His reply upset her; he could see that immediately from the look on her face, but the memories of that night were still painful and routinely he had to repress them, putting them far into the darker recesses of his mind. There was no answer anyway. None that made sense.

"That was when I almost left the force." Trying too late to soften the hardness of his earlier answer, he spoke again. "I think I told you already. Lena refused my resignation and sent me to negotiating school instead."

Despite her obvious frustration at his reticence, Jennifer raised her hand in a comforting gesture, as if she were about to put her fingers on his arm, but at the last minute, she didn't. She pulled them back, and he suffered the loss even though he hadn't felt her touch to begin with.

"I'm sorry," was all she said.

"I am, too," he answered. "Especially for the three officers who died." *And the four little kids.* The images shifted slightly—they never left—and he focused on Jennifer once more. "I believe in Maria. She helped me."

The momentary sympathy that had warmed her dark-brown eyes slowly disappeared. "I'm glad, but I don't think she'd do anything for me. I don't need help, anyway."

She was hurting and didn't even know it. Maria *could* help her. Then he realized how futile it would be to try to persuade Jennifer. She'd made up her mind and he wasn't going to change it, just like he wasn't going to get her to go out with him. Shortly after that, she'd left the party, and he'd watched her walk away without saying another word.

The traffic whizzed along Highway 98 and Beck stood by, looking at his watch one more time. She ought to be coming soon or she was going to be late. Maria hadn't told him, of course, but he'd charmed— then tricked—Sher, the receptionist, into telling him the time of Jennifer's appointment. But she obviously wasn't going to keep the booking Betty Whitmire had made. Disappointment rose inside him. He knew it was pointless, but he'd wanted one more chance.

Beck waited a few more minutes, then he started down the palm-lined sidewalk. His apartment was only a few blocks over, the headquarters of the team down the street in the opposite direction. He'd walked to Maria's, leaving his car at home. As he waited for the light to change, he looked idly around, then stopped. Jennifer stood at the door he'd just left.

She looked angry and upset, and as he stared, she raised one hand and tugged at her dress. She stood in the sunshine a moment longer, then she pushed on the door and went inside.

A BLAST OF FRIGID AIR hit Jennifer as she opened the glass doors of the building that housed Maria Worley's offices. She'd rather be anywhere else on earth than here, in this doctor's office, but Betty hadn't left her a choice.

"You really need to talk to her," the woman had insisted. "I've had two sessions with her myself and she's a lovely person. I want you to do this, Jennifer. For me, please…"

That had been two days ago, on the Monday after the party. Sitting across from Betty's massive desk, Jennifer had wanted to refuse. She'd started to say no, willing to suffer the consequences, whatever they might be, but something in Betty's expression had stopped her. By the time Jennifer had left she'd convinced herself she'd imagined it but for just that one second Betty had actually appeared to care. Jennifer had given in and agreed, but now she was regretting the capitulation more than ever.

Making her way to the seventh floor and then through the maze of suites, she opened the door to the one marked Dr. Maria Worley and stepped inside. The receptionist, who sat at one end behind a small, white desk, looked up as Jennifer approached. "I'm Jennifer Barclay," she said, her stomach fluttering. "I have a three o'clock appointment."

The woman smiled warmly. "Oh, yes, Miss Barclay, the doctor's expecting you. I'll let her know you're here."

Jennifer turned and headed toward a blue couch on the other side of the room, but before she could sit down, the door opposite her opened and Maria Worley stuck her head out. "Jennifer—come on in. I'm glad to see you made it."

As if I had a choice, she thought.

Jennifer greeted the dark-haired woman then followed her down a short hallway to her inner office, a bright, open area with a wall of windows facing south. They weren't directly on the waterfront, but the building towered over the smaller beach houses and condos in front of it, so the view was spectacular. For as far as she could see, emerald green waves rolled in and out, a stretch of pristine white sand stopping their progress with foamy precision. In the distance, past the waves, a parade of sailboats and fishing rigs dotted the horizon, their serpentine line leading backward to the marina just down the road.

It was a peaceful, calm scene, and Jennifer wondered at once if that was why Maria Worley had picked the office. Did she think it would bring serenity to her confused and upset clients? The contrast made Jennifer remember Danny's doctor. A cold, reserved man who'd expressed no opinions of his own, the psychologist had reminded her of a dead fish when she'd visited him once with Danny. His office, in shades of gray and black, had been so stark and bleak it'd scared her. Judging solely by her decor, Maria Worley was a very different kind of doctor.

But that still didn't mean Jennifer wanted to talk to her.

Confronted with two chairs and a couch, Jennifer nervously took one of the plump armchairs and sat down, putting her purse at her feet. To her surprise,

Maria took the sofa, sitting back comfortably on its floral-patterned cushions and even slipping off her shoes to tuck her legs underneath her. They could have been two friends settling in for a chat, only Jennifer knew better. She crossed her arms and waited for Maria to speak.

"You don't want to be here, do you?" The psychologist smiled, her expression taking some of the edge off her bluntness.

"No, I don't." If she was going to be that direct, Jennifer could be, too. "I only came because Betty insisted."

"I know. I told her coerced therapy was never a good idea, but you know Betty...." Maria grinned again. "She has a mind of her own so I just let her make the appointment then counted on having a free hour." She clasped her hands behind her head and leaned back. "Looks like I won't be hitting that sale down at the mall after all, huh?"

The doctor's refreshing openness and almost conspiratorial attitude did just what it was supposed to— lowered Jennifer's emotional barrier. She knew exactly what Maria Worley was doing, but she was so good at it, Jennifer couldn't help herself. She grinned in return. "I could leave now and we could both go."

"That'd be fine with me," Maria laughed. "Reluctant clients are not happy campers. Betty didn't accept my opinion, though."

"She doesn't accept anyone's, but her own. She's not a good listener."

Maria lowered her arms, clasped her hands in her lap and looked at Jennifer. "Do you think Howard French felt that way about her, too? That she didn't listen to him?"

Jennifer shook her head at the frank question. "I don't know, but probably. Betty wasn't kind to Howard. In fact, she was downright mean. The way she talked to him reminded me of my father."

"Why is that?"

Again, Jennifer realized what was happening. She was actually talking, and she hadn't wanted to do that at all. But Maria Worley wasn't like a doctor. She seemed genuinely interested.

"He was a cruel, sadistic person and he belittled everyone he came in contact with. Betty's not *that* bad, but there was just something about the way she spoke to Howard." Jennifer shuddered. "It brought back so many memories."

Maria waited calmly, and Jennifer kept going before she could stop herself. "He gave my brother an especially hard time, and I guess that's one of the reasons Howard's death affected me so much. They were a lot alike, my brother and Howard, and I had wanted to help him, too."

"Help him, too?"

Jennifer glanced up. "My brother died in an accident when I was a child."

"I'm sorry to hear that. How old was he? How old were you?"

"He was sixteen. I was ten."

Something in Jennifer's attitude must have come through. "Were you present when it happened?"

Jennifer closed her eyes then opened them after a minute. "I was standing right beside him...and I didn't do a thing."

"Are you saying you think you could have prevented what happened?"

"Of course."

"Are you sure?"

The doctor's words reminded Jennifer of Wanda's. She looked up and met the woman's dark eyes. "I always thought I could."

The doctor nodded. "Children do that."

Jennifer's tongue stuck to the roof of her mouth. She felt as though she'd bitten into a biscuit made only of flour. She finally managed to speak. "Children do what?"

"Feel responsible," Maria answered. "Look at the kids in your classroom. Think of the last one whose parents divorced, and I bet you'll see what I'm talking about. Unless they're reassured repeatedly, they always believe the divorce is their fault, no matter what."

Jennifer sat in silence. There was nothing to say.

"So it's completely understandable you'd feel that way about your brother." Maria shrugged casually.

"But I'm sure you know that's not the case. You wouldn't be the terrific teacher Beck told me you are without seeing that for the fallacy it is."

Jennifer nodded slowly. *Of course. You're right.* The words wedged themselves in her still-dry throat and refused to come out. None of this was news to her, but she'd never applied the theory to herself.

"Look, you really don't have to stay here if you'd rather not. I'll tell Betty we met and leave it at that." Maria swung her feet to the floor. "Whatever you want."

Jennifer stared at the woman. She had a kind face and as she waited patiently for Jennifer to answer, she wondered how many tears had been shed in this office by someone sitting in the very chair where Jennifer now was. How did Maria Worley absorb them without drowning? How did she deal with the pain? What would she say that could help?

Could she end Jennifer's nightmares?

The decision was an impulsive one, but it felt exactly right. "I think I'd rather stay."

Maria smiled warmly and settled back into the couch. "Then I'm all yours. Let's talk…."

FORTY-FIVE MINUTES LATER, the doors to the office building opened and Jennifer came outside. The sun was just beginning to head westward, and in the pale-yellow streaks that heralded its exit, her skin turned to gold. She wore a navy blue jumper—nothing like the white sundress from the party—but the simple lines seemed made for her, elegant and classy. Beck stared at her for a few seconds, almost unable to move, then he realized she was walking down the street toward her Toyota. If he didn't hustle, he'd miss her. He jumped up from the bench where he'd been waiting and crossed the street to cut her off.

Her eyes widened when she saw him and she stopped abruptly. "Beck! What are you doing here?"

He thought about lying, but couldn't, and that surprised him so much for a moment, he was actually at a loss for words. "I knew you had an appointment," he said finally, opting for the simple truth and nothing more. "I wanted to see how it went for you."

She started to answer, but he interrupted, speaking quickly before she could think up an excuse to dash away. "There's a juice vendor down the street. Walk down that way with me and have something. We'll talk."

"Beck, I don't—"

He ignored her protest and took her elbow instead. "It's not a date," he said. "A fruit smoothie after work doesn't count."

She looked up at him and he could see she'd been crying. And suddenly it hit him. He was attracted to Jennifer—had been since the moment he'd seen her—but now it was more than just that.

"I'd like to hear what the doc had to say." Rubbing the inside of her elbow with his thumb, he felt the silk of her skin. "We'll have something to drink and you can tell me."

She pulled her arm away, then nervously reached up to touch her hair. The dark curls were piled haphazardly on top of her head with longer ringlets hanging down around her face. "There's nothing *to* tell," she said. "I talked to her about my nightmares. And we discussed my family, spoke some about Betty. I had a problem the other day at the grocery store. I guess you'd call it a flashback, and I told her about that." She shook her head. "It was boring stuff, really. You wouldn't want to hear it."

"Try me."

She seemed tempted for a moment, then she shook her head again and even took a step back. "I'm sorry, I really can't. Today's Wednesday. I always visit my mother on Wednesdays."

She said the words so precisely he understood immediately. Her life was ruled by a schedule, by bells, by teaching plans. She didn't like disruptions or changes and all the hints he'd seen of this before now made sense. Another piece of the puzzle fell into place.

"C'mon. Five minutes," he said. "That's all. Then we'll drive to Seacrest with my red lights flashing, how's that?"

She looked alarmed, her brown eyes rounding. "We?"

"I've got some free time. I'd love to meet your mother."

"Oh, no. I don't think—"

"Jennifer…"

She fell silent.

"Let me be friendly, please." He looked down at her and this time he did lie. "That's all I want. Just to be your friend."

She didn't know what to say. He could see the conflict cross her expression.

"I think you could use one," he said. "And I know I could."

She seemed to consider his answer, then she nodded slowly. "All right. Five minutes, and that's it. I have to leave."

They walked down the sidewalk toward the yellow-and-white-striped umbrella that marked the juice stand, Beck wondering with each step what it would take to earn her trust. What had been a vague suspicion before turned into a more concrete notion. There was more to her lack of trust than the incident with Howard French. It went back a lot further than that and way beyond Beck. What was the problem?

Esther, the older woman working the stand, grinned at him as she filled their orders. Leaning over the counter, she nodded toward Jennifer. "Very nice, Mr. Beck. I'm glad you've found yourself a lady friend. You treat her good, now."

Beck glanced over at Jennifer and smiled. "I will if she'll let me, Esther."

Jennifer's blush deepened.

Paying the woman behind the cart, Beck steered Jennifer to a shaded table a few feet away, then pulled out her chair. When he pushed it in, he couldn't help but stare at the back of her neck. Shorter tendrils of her chestnut hair lay along the curved line of her spine, and all at once he imagined pressing his mouth along its ridge. *Get a grip,* he told himself, then he ignored the advice. The spot would be warm and tender and taste slightly salty.

Jennifer spoke first. "You come here a lot?"

He grinned widely. "I stop on my way to work every morning. Esther's always giving me advice of some kind."

"You live nearby?"

"Just down the block. I have an apartment close to the beach. I like to do a little surf fishing now and then, so it's nice to be around the water."

She asked the questions with determination, as if she were bound to make pleasant conversation and nothing deeper, then disappear after the allotted five minutes. "Are you from Destin?"

"No," he answered slowly, just as determined to draw the time out. "I grew up in the north, near Rochester, New York. Hated the cold and the snow and the sleet, and as soon as I could I headed south. I wandered around for a while, and ended up here."

"Is that when you joined the SWAT team?"

He shook his head. "I was a street cop for a long time, then I met Lena at a guy's retirement party. She convinced me I'd be good for the team and that I'd enjoy the work. I got my training and joined up shortly after that."

She put her elbows on the table, trying to seem casual, but failing. "Is it hard? What you do?"

The ocean breeze grabbed one of her curls and sent it flying into her eyes. She lifted her hand, but he beat her to it, reaching across the table and pulling the strand away first. He rubbed it between his thumb and finger for just a second before tucking it behind her ear. The curl felt as soft and silky as her skin.

He put away the sensation and thought about her question. "It's not the easiest thing in the world, but I enjoy helping people and saving lives." He paused. "I know you still have questions about what happened at the school, but I believe in my work. I hope that's not why you won't see me."

She followed his fingers with her own, securing the curl better. Her perfume was light and airy and smelled of lilacs as it drifted over to him. "I *do* still have some questions, but it goes beyond that."

He leaned across the plastic tabletop, dropping all pretense of a casual conversation. "Then tell me. Why won't you give me a chance?"

She licked her lips. They were lined with the same soft-pink shade he'd noticed that first day. "I have my life organized,'' she said slowly. "It's just the way I like it. Calm, serene, planned. Every day I know what I'm going to do and I do it. That's how I want it. You live a totally different way, Beck.''

Her words only reinforced the realization he'd had moments before; she had to have her life ordered. He understood the need, but why did that prevent her from seeing him? "And?" he said.

She lifted her gaze. "And I don't want to get involved with someone who lives the way you must. Because of my father's work, our lives were filled with total confusion when I was growing up, confusion and secrets, too many secrets. When I got old enough to handle things on my own, I promised myself I wouldn't live that way again. Ever. It's too crazy.''

A seagull cried out overhead and Beck shook his head. "Life *is* crazy, Jennifer. You can't hide and pretend otherwise.''

"I'm not hiding!" she said hotly.

"Then go out with me," he said. "Live a little. Vary your routine and see your mother at six instead of five." He reached across the table and took her hands in his. "I promise you…the universe will keep spinning and you won't fall off the planet. Life will go on if your plans are changed.''

As soon as he'd said the words, Beck knew he'd made a mistake. Her expression went chilly and she pulled her fingers away. Pushing her chair back until the metal legs screeched against the concrete side-walk, she rose angrily. Before she could speak, though, a woman approached the table. Beck hadn't heard her coming, and afterward, he cursed himself for being so unaware. If he'd known what was about to happen, he could have reacted faster. As it was, he had no forewarning to rely upon, only instinct. She was well dressed and posed no physical threat, but Beck stood immediately. Something was wrong.

With an expression of pure anger, she glared an-grily at Jennifer. "I'm having you fired," she snarled furiously. "You're the worst excuse for a teacher I've ever seen and I'm going to make sure this whole town knows it!"

CHAPTER NINE

"NANCY!" Jennifer retreated a step involuntarily, her chair scraping the sidewalk again, even more loudly this time. "Wh-what's wrong? What are you talking about?"

Nancy Thomas, the mother of one of Jennifer's students, continued to stare at Jennifer with a venomous expression. "You're what's wrong!" she cried. "What kind of teacher are you to let this happen?"

"What are you talking about?" Jennifer sent a helpless glance in Beck's direction. "I don't understand.... Please calm yourself!"

"You almost got my baby killed. Don't go telling me to calm down! You let a man with a gun come into your classroom. How could you? You're supposed to protect those poor children."

Jennifer stared at the distraught woman, her heart knocking against her ribs as she searched her brain for a way to reply. A single parent, Nancy worked long hours for a local brokerage firm and traveled constantly. Her ex-husband devoted an equal amount of time to his dental practice. Matthew spent more time with a housekeeper than he did with his parents.

"Nancy, please..."

Jennifer started around the table, but Beck intercepted her, putting himself protectively between her and Nancy Thomas.

"Let's just all cool down here," he said pleasantly. His voice was affable but at the same time, Jennifer couldn't help but see that his blue eyes were assessing the other woman intently. "Nancy, is it? Nancy with an *I* or with a *y?*"

She looked at him blankly, thrown off base by his question. "With a *y.* Who are you?"

"I'm Beck Winters. I'm a friend of Jennifer's but I happen to work with the Emerald Coast SWAT team."

"Then you're just as guilty as she is!" Nancy said loudly. "My child was in that classroom. He saw someone get killed! What kind of place is this? How did that idiot get inside, and why wasn't he arrested before this happened? What kind of cop are you?"

Beck spoke in a low and reasonable voice. "I don't think you understand the situation—"

"I understand it all right. I understand my child was in harm's way and you did what cops always do. You shot first and asked questions later."

The unfairness of her accusation was too much to bear. It didn't matter that the stinging words were awfully close to Jennifer's own feelings, Nancy Thomas had no right to attack Beck, none whatsoever. He'd done the best he could, and responding angrily,

Jennifer began to defend him. "You don't know what you're saying, Nancy. Officer Winters did everything he could to—"

Nancy swung around and faced her furiously. "Don't you dare stand up for him. You should have stopped this whole thing before it happened. Why didn't you—"

"That's enough!" Beck's voice rumbled across the outdoor area. A group of older people standing near one of the flower beds turned and looked. "Lower your voice, ma'am, and collect yourself."

She started to speak again, then all at once, she collapsed. Beck had no choice but to catch her. She would have fallen otherwise. He wrapped his huge arms around her, and she let out a sob, clinging to him tightly, crying in earnest now.

"I—I was out of town," she hiccuped. "My ex called and told me what happened, but I couldn't come back. Matthew could have been killed and I wasn't even here! I—I can't believe it!"

A wave of sympathy replaced Jennifer's anger. She understood now, understood Nancy completely. Unable to return, she'd felt helpless. Her guilt had been building all this time.

"It's okay," Beck murmured. "It's all right." Looking over Nancy's head into Jennifer's eyes, Beck nodded toward a chair. Jennifer scrambled to bring it closer and when she'd done so, Beck eased his way toward it. Gently he lowered Nancy Thomas's trembling form into the seat.

"But your son is okay." He spoke in a kind voice and looked directly into her eyes. "Your son is perfectly fine, and even if you had been here, you wouldn't have been able to do anything for him. Not at that moment."

"B-but he saw someone k-killed! It's just too horrible!" She jerked her eyes to Jennifer's face. "Why didn't you stop him—"

"Whoa, whoa…"

Just as it had been when he'd talked to Jennifer over the phone that horrible day, Beck's voice was firm but compassionate as he interrupted Nancy Thomas. Hearing those calming tones, everything rushed back and all at once Jennifer turned faint, suddenly feeling as weak and strange as she had last week in the grocery store. She sensed the color leave her face and she, too, sat down.

Beck was focused on the upset woman, but he glanced at Jennifer. Seeing her obvious distress, he gave her a reassuring look with those startling blue eyes. Everything would be all right, they said, and she didn't have to do anything but let him handle it.

He turned back to Nancy. "Miss Barclay did everything she could in that classroom to avert disaster. In fact, if she hadn't been there, no telling what would have happened. You owe her a debt of gratitude, not a hard time." He stopped and sent another glance in

Jennifer's direction. The words were directed to the woman in front of him, but Jennifer understood who he was really speaking to. "She did the right thing every step of the way," he said. "I helped, but she saved lives, and we should all be grateful."

Beck's praise warmed something deep inside her, and even as she fought the sensation, Jennifer felt the last bit of her resistance melt under his approving look. How could she be embarrassed and ridiculously pleased at the same time? To cover her confusion, she looked back at Nancy, who wore a doubting expression of uncertainty.

Jennifer took one of the woman's hands in hers. "Nancy, please, if I'd known you were gone, I would have called you. Betty never told me. I had no idea. Matthew didn't say anything, either."

Her anger deflating under Jennifer's sympathy, Nancy Thomas's eyes filled with tears of remorse. "I was in London. There was an emergency and I ran out to catch a flight that morning. I didn't even kiss Matthew goodbye before I left. I was on my way to the school when I saw you sitting here. I stopped the car. I was just so upset and scared and..." She took a deep, ragged breath, glancing at Beck and then Jennifer. "I—I'm sorry, Jennifer, really sorry. I guess I just went crazy with the thought of what could have happened."

"I understand." Her stomach quaking, Jennifer

nodded. She looked at Beck and spoke again. "Believe me, I understand."

"GIVE ME YOUR KEYS."

They were walking down the sidewalk a half hour later, heading for Jennifer's car. "I'm going to drive you to Seacrest," Beck said. "You have no business behind the wheel as upset as you are."

"I'm fine, really."

He lifted his eyebrows. "That shade of white is your normal color?" He shook his head. "I don't think so, Jennifer. Let me drive."

She answered as they reached her car, her keys in her hand. "But I'm okay," she insisted. "Perfectly all right."

He didn't bother to answer. Instead, he reached over, took her hand in his, and pried open her fingers. It didn't take much effort. She was clearly shaken and didn't have the energy to resist him. "You're upset," he said. "And rightfully so. Let me drive you over there, then I'll catch a taxi back to the station. I don't want to see you have an accident."

She didn't say a word; she simply stood there, beside her car, her hand cradled in his. "Are you sure?"

He squeezed her fingers gently. "I wouldn't have offered if I wasn't."

Her eyes filled suddenly and she shook her head. "I can't believe that! Poor Nancy. She must have felt so horrible when she heard the news."

A single tear escaped her right eye and Beck lifted his finger to stop it. Beneath his palm, her sun-warmed skin was smooth and soft. The sensation made him hungry for more, but he satisfied himself with this meager taste, afraid he'd scare her off if he brought her as close to him as he wanted. She was feeling unsure of herself and no one could understand that better than him. Flashbacks, nightmares? He'd suspected as much, but having her confess to the problems made them more real. They were clear signs of PTSD. Instead of worrying about herself, though, she was concerned for a woman who'd just tried to assault her. Suddenly he wanted to wrap Jennifer up in a blanket and protect her from everything... including herself.

"You handled yourself well back there." He shook his head in amazement. "I think she might have decked you, if I hadn't been there."

"I know," she said. "But I understand, too. If my child had been in that classroom, I would have been just as upset."

He rubbed his thumb gently over her cheek. "But you did everything you could. And the kids did fine because of you. You have nothing to regret, if that's what you're thinking. You handled that situation better than a lot of cops would have, believe me."

Her eyes shimmered. "Are you telling me the truth?"

"Why would I lie?"

She reached up and put her hand on his wrist. Her grip was surprisingly strong. "You told me once you'd lie to save lives. Why not lie to make me feel better?"

"This is different. And you'll just have to trust that I'm telling the truth."

She blinked, her long, curled eyelashes lowering then sweeping up again. Small beads of moisture dotted her upper lip as the dying sun beat down on them. "I don't have a lot of experience with trust."

He tightened his fingers along her jaw. "Then maybe it's time to get some."

JENNIFER SAT in the seat beside Beck as he maneuvered the Toyota out of the parking spot and into the stream of traffic. It was a small car and he filled the front seat, just as he did most of the places he occupied. It was more than his physical size, although that was definitely a factor. He filled it with his presence, his strength, his attitude. Jennifer glanced over at him, her eyes going to his capable hands as they gripped the steering wheel. Jennifer's cheek felt hot from his caress. What would it feel like to have those hands touch her more intimately?

She closed her eyes and leaned her head against the headrest of the car, grateful all at once that Beck had insisted on driving. She felt drained and exhausted. Seeing Maria Worley had been her biggest worry this morning, but now that seemed like a lifetime ago, and petty, as well. The talk with Maria had actually proven to be the best part of Jennifer's day!

Beck had cooled Nancy's anger almost instantly. Thinking back on the situation, Jennifer marveled at the way he'd handled the woman. Firm yet gentle. It was easy to see how he could calm someone even more upset and angry, and all at once, her eyes were opened as they'd never been before. She couldn't help but wonder how things would have ended if Howard had actually talked to Beck instead of using her, then she put the thought aside. What good would it do to dwell on it now?

They arrived at the nursing home a short ten minutes later. Beck pulled the car into the nearest shaded parking spot and killed the engine, the scent of honeysuckle and salty sea air riding the summer breeze into the open windows of the car. As the motor ticked down, Jennifer turned in the seat to look at him.

"Thank you," she said simply.

"You're welcome," he said. "But for what?"

"For doing what you did back there. For taking care of things."

He tipped an imaginary hat. "Just doing my duty, ma'am."

"I'm serious," she said. "I really do appreciate it. I think about the negatives of what you do, the secrets, the danger, the unsettled nature of it all, but if you hadn't been there, I'm not sure how I would have dealt with Nancy.''

He reached across the seat and put his hand on her shoulder. In the shaded light of where they sat, his eyes almost glowed, and for a passing second, she had the ridiculous thought that he might be about to kiss her. She stiffened while deep down inside she knew she wanted nothing more.

''Does this mean you'll go out with me?''

''You're relentless, aren't you?''

''I never give up,'' he agreed. ''And now you owe me. I saved you from a pretty dramatic moment. From the viewpoint of a negotiator, I deserve something in return.''

He waited, her unspoken answer hanging between them.

''Well?'' he said.

He was right, but if she admitted that, she'd admit more, if only to herself. And she wasn't ready for more just yet. ''I'll consider the possibility,'' she said.

He ran the back of one finger over her cheek, then dropped his hand. ''I guess right now that's the best I can hope for.''

IT WAS PAST six o'clock and the halls of the nursing home were almost empty, the smell of pot roast and mashed potatoes a clue as to where everyone was. Jennifer led Beck to the nurses' station and leaned over the counter to pick up the phone and call a cab.

He reached out and stopped her at the very last minute.

"I really would like to meet your mother," he said. "Would it upset her to see a stranger?"

Jennifer hesitated, then put the phone back down. "I don't think so. If you had on your uniform, that'd be another story."

He tilted his head quizzically and she explained.

When she finished, he nodded, his expression thoughtful. "No offense, but your father must have really been a bastard."

Jennifer smiled grimly. "That just about sums it up. He punished my mother by withholding his affection, but he saved his cruelest taunts for my brother. He pretty much ignored me."

"I want to know more about Danny."

Something tightened inside her. "There's nothing to tell—"

He reached out and put his fingers across her lips. "Don't ever try to lie to a liar," he said quietly. "We always know."

Her breath stopped, but she found herself nodding. There was nothing else she could do with his touch on her mouth and his eyes boring into hers.

"This isn't the time or the place, but I want to know." He took his finger away. "Fair warning."

Concentrating on Beck, Jennifer failed to notice Wanda's arrival. Only after the nurse coughed, ever so delicately, did Jennifer realize she was standing right beside her. She came to with a start.

"W-Wanda! I didn't see you," she stuttered.

"I noticed," she answered dryly. Looking up at Beck, she extended her hand. "I'm Wanda La-Fleur…and you're Beck Winters."

"That's right." He took her hand carefully in his and shook it once. Jennifer was surprised. Most men his size squeezed and pumped, but Beck wasn't like most men.

"Are we having an old folks' breakout?" Wanda asked, raising one eyebrow. "Somebody call in the SWAT team over the mashed potatoes again?"

Beck laughed. "Not that I know of." He glanced down at Jennifer and his blue eyes seemed warm all at once. She told herself it was the lighting over the desk. "I brought Jennifer to see her mom. I didn't want her endangering the citizens of Destin."

Wanda put her hands on her hips. "You speedin' again, girl? I thought we talked about that."

Jennifer shook her head. "You wouldn't believe it if I tried to explain. Let's just save it for later."

"Okay." Her black eyes turned serious. "Might be better anyway. Your mama's not having too good a day. In fact," she looked up at Beck, "I'm not really sure this would be the time for a new visitor. She's pretty confused."

Beck nodded. "I understand completely." Again he looked at Jennifer. "Why don't I just wait out here? When you finish, we can decide what to do later.''

Feeling Wanda's eyes on her face, Jennifer answered quickly. ''No, no. Please don't hang around just for me. I might be a while. Why don't you go ahead and call a cab?''

''I'll wait.''

His answer held no room for argument, and Jennifer couldn't help herself; a warm flush of anticipation came over her at the thought of what *later* might bring. ''Okay,'' she answered.

''Good.'' Without any further warning, he bent down and brushed her cheek with his lips, then turned and walked away.

Jennifer stood silently in a state of shock. The kiss was totally casual, something you'd expect from a friend or a cousin, but she felt it hit her in three places at once. Her cheek at his touch. Her mind at his actions. Her heart at his sweetness. He really did care.

Under her breath, Wanda spoke beside her. ''Whooeee... That is one hunk of a man, honey.'' She glanced sideways at Jennifer and grinned. ''What trick are you trying to pull telling me you're not interested? You look like you just got hit by a truck.''

''I feel like I did, too.''

Wanda took her by the arm and led her down the hallway. ''Then go with it, baby. Just go with it.''

THINKING OF JENNIFER, Beck headed for the blue plaid sofa in one corner of the waiting room. He probably shouldn't have kissed her like that, but it had seemed like the right thing to do. She'd looked so upset, so overwhelmed by everything that had happened to her, he'd wanted to let her know she didn't have to carry it all on her shoulders. He didn't know if the message got through or not, but he could still smell her perfume and still feel the softness of her cheek beneath his lips. It'd been worth it for that if nothing else.

Crossing a small area rug, he walked to the couch, but he didn't get a chance to sit. The beeper at his belt began to vibrate and sound just as he lowered himself to the cushions. It only took one look at the readout to know he had a problem, and he sprang up immediately. The flashing code, in bright-red numbers, told it all.

Priority One. Priority One. An address followed.

He didn't take the time to try to find Jennifer. He couldn't. A message like that meant every member of the team was needed and needed immediately. He hit the corridor running, the startled nurse's aide looking up as he streaked past the desk. "Tell Jennifer Barclay I had to leave," he yelled, throwing the words over his shoulder and not even looking back. "I'll call her as soon as I can."

Digging into his pocket for his key ring, he ran along the sidewalk. By the time he reached the parking lot, he realized his problem.

He didn't have his keys because he didn't have his truck. The realization didn't stop him; it couldn't. Someone's life was in danger, maybe more than just one "someone's." He sprinted toward the Toyota, clutching Jennifer's key chain, and two seconds later, he was in her car, speeding away from the nursing home.

JENNIFER CLOSED the door behind her as she entered her mother's room. She was exhausted and completely drained, but she was here. It was Wednesday and she was here.

The lights were dim and low, the only sound coming from the television set located on the wall above the bathroom entrance. Her mother was already asleep. When Jennifer and Beck had arrived, she'd been upset and worried over everything that had happened, but now she was even more unnerved. Wanda had explained as they'd walked down the corridor about the bad day Nadine had had.

"I don't know exactly how to tell you this," the nurse had said, "but we lost your mama for a while today. She was nowhere to be found."

Jennifer had stopped so fast, her heels had streaked the polished linoleum floor. "What?"

"It's true," Wanda said, shaking her head and sighing. "I can't believe it, but she was somewhere other than her bedroom or the patio, and we still don't know where. We were gettin' frantic, then here she

came, ambling down the hallway tryin' to see what
all the fuss was about. I damned near had a heart
attack, Jennifer. I don't know how I could have called
you and told you that, especially on top of everything
else.''

Jennifer closed her eyes, the hall swimming for just
a minute. When she opened them again, Wanda
looked so miserable, Jennifer ended up consoling her.
''Oh, Wanda, it's not your fault. You can't watch her
every second of the day.''

Regret filled her dark eyes. ''But I'm supposed to.
That's what you pay us for.''

''Where do you think she went?''

''I have no idea, but not off the grounds, I'm sure.
She couldn't have. She wasn't gone ten minutes.''

Jennifer patted Wanda's arm. ''Did you ask her
where she'd been?''

''Oh, yeah, we asked.''

''And?''

''She said she'd been to visit your brother. Said
Danny had called and she'd gone to see him.''

For the third time that day, Jennifer felt her world
shake a little, a small temor but one she couldn't ignore. ''Oh, Wanda...''

''I know, honey, I know.''

Jennifer shook her head. ''What are we going to
do?''

''We're not going to do anything, except keep a
closer eye on her.'' Her accent deepened and her

voice went soft. "She's getting worse, baby. She's having more days than not when she's losing everything. I haven't wanted to say anything, but you might need to consider moving her to the more restricted wing of the home. They *can* watch her closer over there, you know."

"I don't want to do that." Jennifer looked at her friend in dismay. She didn't bother to list all the reasons why. Money. Time. Effort. She only voiced the most important one. "It'd upset her so. She loves you and she has her routine established with everyone else...."

Wanda interrupted with a shake of her head. "Sweetheart, she didn't have a clue who *I* was this morning and she's never done that before."

Not knowing what to say, Jennifer stared at Wanda with dismay. Nadine always knew Wanda, even when she didn't recognize Jennifer. This *was* troubling.

Wanda gave her a quick hug, then Jennifer had gone inside. Walking to the edge of her mother's bed now, Jennifer looked down and cursed herself for the sudden rush of resentment that overcame her.

She was an awful person and a terrible daughter.

She didn't want to be there. She didn't want to have to face this problem—a mother who didn't know who she was or even where she was—and she didn't want to deal with all the dilemmas that came with it.

She didn't want any of it.

Her nice orderly life was falling apart, and even the

solution that popped into her head was an answer that made no sense. How could she want what added the most to her crazy state of mind?

It made no sense, absolutely none, but all that was comforting Jennifer, the *one* thing that made her feel better, was the knowledge that Beck was down the hall waiting for her, his arms a refuge she could take at any time.

CHAPTER TEN

"WHAT HAVE WE GOT?" They were in the War Wagon, Beck struggling into his vest as he made his way to the back where Lena sat.

"A domestic violence with multiple weapons." She glanced in his direction as he spoke, then focused on the fax coming through the machine. "Caught the call from the Panama City Beach guys. Apparently the suspect is a frequent client of theirs. He's been in and out of county for petty stuff, but this is the first time it's been this serious. He's high on something and he's inside, waving a knife in one hand and a gun in the other. We can't tell if the wife is a hostage or what."

Beck peered out the window of the motor home toward the tiny beachfront shack about a hundred yards from where they were parked. In the growing dusk, it was hard to see the details, but he didn't need too much light; he knew the neighborhood. The single street ran perpendicular to the beach, and the houses along its rutted path were mostly frame, all run-down, and completely worthless compared to the land they sat on. Lena had already killed the power to the homes so the stretch of road was empty and quiet, but at the end, he caught a flash of white motion now and again—the phosphorescence of the waves crashing on the sandy beach.

In her usual concise way, Lena gave him more details, outlining the positions of the rest of the team and explaining what had happened. A frantic 911 from the neighbors had brought the beat cops out, but when they'd tried to approach the residence, numerous shots had been fired, inside and outside the house. Nodding his head at the narrative, Beck picked up the phone and dialed the number she had handed him.

No answer. He dialed again, an empty ringing sounding in his ear as Lena spoke.

"Where were you when you caught the call?"

"I was at Seacrest."

"Seacrest? The old folks' home?"

He disconnected the line, then punched the redial almost immediately. "I think the proper term is *retirement facility*."

She shook her head impatiently. "Whatever. What were you doing there?"

"I was with Jennifer Barclay. We were visiting her mother."

He started to say more, but all of his instincts went on sudden alert as the phone was answered. No one spoke, but he heard a small sound, almost nothing but enough to trigger his attention. "Hello? Hello?" More silence was his only answer. His stomach roiled as he remembered the last time this had happened, when Howard French had refused to speak with him. Beck swallowed to get past the memory. "This is Beck Winters with the Emerald Coast SWAT team. Who am I talking to, please?"

He glanced at Lena. She had raised one eyebrow as if to say "What's the deal?" He shrugged his shoulders and scribbled on a notepad. "No answer."

She nodded her silent acknowledgment. They couldn't risk a conversation being overheard without knowing who had answered the phone. She wrote something on the pad and shoved it toward him. "Any background noise?"

Beck pressed the receiver closer to his ear and closed his eyes, concentrating. There might have been something…he caught just a hint of a breath, the fleeting impression that someone was there, but it was nothing more than that. He could have just as easily imagined it. He opened his eyes and shook his head. He didn't want to lose the open line and had no idea if anyone was even listening, but he began to talk, a rambling introduction with questions interspersed, hoping against hope one would elicit a response from the person on the other end.

"I'm with the Emerald Coast SWAT team," he repeated, "and we're here to help you and help whoever's in there with you. We understand you had a little problem tonight and we don't want anyone getting hurt so we came out to see what's going on. Are you there..?'' He rummaged through the notes he'd taken while Lena had explained the situation. ''Are you there, Fred?''

No answer. Beck remembered Jennifer as she'd looked just after the hostage incident. He wasn't about to end another one that way this soon. He gripped the phone tighter and stared at the notes, using his standard opening ploy—saying something about the perp's name. People always responded when you talked about their name. Nothing was more personal.

''Fred, I see your last name is Mikeouski. I had a buddy in college named Mikeouski. He was from Long Island. You wouldn't be from there, would you?'' He made his voice friendly. ''That'd be a hoot, wouldn't it? His first name was T.C. Well, I mean his *name* was Thomas Charleston, but he couldn't stand that so we called him T.C. He's not your cousin or anything, is he?'' *Answer me,* he wanted to scream. *Just say something so I know you're in there and you haven't blown your wife to kingdom come.*

The name trick didn't work. Beck stared at the man's house. Near the northwest corner, by one tire of a weary-looking pickup truck, a quick movement grabbed his attention. Beck tensed before he realized what he was seeing, then he spoke quickly. ''Hey, Fred. I see your dog in the yard. Damn, he's a great-looking retriever. You a hunter, Fred? Ducks? Deer? What?'' Cradling the phone between his shoulder and jaw, he picked up the binoculars on the desk and trained them on the truck. There *was* a gun rack across the back window but it held a fishing rod. ''I bet you like to fish better than hunt, huh? You got a boat somewhere? You take the dog out with you? Those retrievers do love the water, don't they?''

He took a deep breath and prayed for an answer. Anything. A grunt would have worked, but nothing came down the telephone line. Not even a buzz. He could tell he was still connected, but that was all. Lena caught his eye and just shook her head. In situations like this, there was nothing they could do, but hang on. Thank God, there weren't any children inside.

Beck closed his eyes, rested his elbows on the desk and started to talk again. ''When I was kid I had a dog like that. Boy, did that dog love to hunt. I named him Bojangles, kinda dumb name, maybe, but I was just a kid and I'd heard the song so...''

Two hours later, he was going hoarse and running out of even inane things to say. Lena had written him so many notes they had piled up over the desk like snow and were drifting to the floor. Finally, she handed him this one.

This is dragging on too long. Front window. Right side.

He nodded at the cryptic message and continued to speak. Sometimes the only thing they had left was to shake the guy up. Breaking out a window was one of the simplest options. The unexpected noise and destruction was the diversion that convinced some folks to talk...or walk.

But it didn't this time.

The sound of fracturing glass came over the phone line, but it came by itself. No cursing, no call of surprise. Nothing. Beck looked up at Lena and shook his head when she stepped back into the wagon. Pulling a piece of paper toward him, he scribbled furiously. *Mirrors?*

She pulled her microphone closer and spoke. A few seconds later, Beck watched as a long pole was inserted through the now open window. At the end of the rod was a mirror. Beck continued to talk. He didn't think he was making sense now. No one would after this length of time.

Lena pressed her earphone closer, then her expression changed abruptly and she spoke out loud, her voice disbelieving. "Dammit to hell! Are you sure, Hood? Absolutely sure?"

Beck fell silent, his throat stinging.

A second later, she ripped off her headset and stared wearily at him. Outside, the team started in. They weren't doing an assault, but merely a cautionary entry. Swarming over the porch, they called out, then crashed through the door.

"Tell me...." he said painfully, knowing already.

She looked out the window and didn't speak.

He lowered the phone, but still held on to it. He

couldn't hang up. He couldn't break the connection. His fingers refused to make the move. Covering the mouthpiece with his hand, he spoke again, his voice so hoarse it was hard to understand. "Both of them?"

With her back to him, she nodded once.

He cursed loudly, then threw down the receiver. Racing outside, he stumbled in the darkness toward the house, knowing all the time speed no longer mattered.

And it hadn't for some time.

He careened into the living room. Most of the team were near the back door where a man's body was on the floor. Death had already claimed him, rigor mortis stiffening his legs and arms, his face pasty and grey. He'd been dead for hours, probably shot himself right after the beat cops had come. A familiar clutch of dismay swept over Beck, but the groaning burden of failure didn't really hit until his eyes searched further.

He saw the phone first, then he saw her. Sprawled on the floor, the woman looked as if she'd been trying to get away from her dying husband. Beck assessed the situation without even thinking hard. The man had attacked her, then shot himself…only she didn't die—at first. Her hand was wrapped around the phone cord. She was the one who'd answered. Beck's eyes followed the coiled line to the receiver lying near her ear. She'd been listening to him until the end, but she hadn't been able to answer Beck's stupid questions or even call for help.

Her husband had slit her throat.

HAD HE GONE for a walk?

Jennifer came back into the waiting room and when she didn't see Beck right away, she assumed he'd gotten bored. She took a quick tour around the wing that housed her mother, but he was nowhere around so pushing open the double glass doors, she stepped outside. The air was dense and salty, the forerunner of fog. She made her way through it slowly, taking the winding gravel path that circled the home. Five minutes later she was back where she started and still no sign of Beck.

Hesitating in front of the building, Jennifer actually shook her head at the thought that barged into her brain like an unwanted guest. He wouldn't have, she argued with herself. He wouldn't have just left. He would have found her first and told her. Or at the very least, he would have told Pamela. The nurse's aide had been at the station just around the corner from the waiting room the whole time. It wouldn't have taken two minutes to tell her if he'd had an emergency.

Her feet moved without instructions from her brain, but when she found herself in the parking lot, all Jennifer could do was stare blankly at the empty space where her car had been. No, she thought illogically, this can't be. He wouldn't have.

But the facts were before her. No car. No Beck. No "later."

She couldn't bear the onslaught of disappointment that came over her. If she did acknowledge it, then she admitted to herself she was falling for Beck, and she couldn't do that. So instead she got angry. A red flush started at the base of her neck and worked its hot way up her throat to her cheeks. It was still heating her face when she slammed back into the home a few minutes later.

Wanda's startled eyes met Jennifer's over the curved Formica of the nurse's station. "Whoa, girl! What's up with you?"

"He left me," she said between clenched teeth. "Beck took my car and left me."

Wanda frowned, three dark lines dividing her forehead. "Are you sure? I didn't see him leave."

"Well, unless he's invisible as well as invincible, he's gone and so is my car." She put her hands on her hips and shook her head, muttering, "Is Pamela around? Maybe he said something to her...."

"Well, he must have gotten a call. I can't imagine—"

"Are you talking about that man who was with you?" Drawing Jennifer's attention, the aide stepped into the hallway from the linen closet, shutting the door behind her and speaking. "He *did* have to leave. He asked me to tell you, but I've been busy in Mrs. Becker's room. He said he'd call you."

"What happened?"

The young girl shook her head. "I dunno. But he ran out in a big hurry."

Jennifer's earlier disappointment mushroomed. "He got a call."

Wanda came from around the station to stare at Jennifer. Her expression was sympathetic, but pragmatic. "The man's a cop. What do you expect?"

Wanda was right, but Jennifer's regret was so overwhelming she couldn't stand it. She answered unreasonably, knowing her reply sounded foolish. "The least he could have done was find me first."

"Oh, good grief! Come on! What if he'd taken that kind of time before showing up at your school? You woulda been countin' the minutes with that gun at your throat!"

"How long would it take to find me?"

"Too long," Wanda answered. "And you know it." She shook her head, her black hair shining under the lights over the desk. "You're acting like one of your kids! Just give me a minute and I'll drive you home."

She started to say thanks, then Jennifer hesitated. Beck didn't know where she lived, or have her phone number. It was unlisted. How would he return her car? She looked at the aid with a frown. "Did he say he'd come back here or...?"

The girl shook her head. "All he said was he'd call you. That's it."

Facing Wanda again, Jennifer made her up mind. "I think I'll stay here. He doesn't have my number or address. He'll probably come back and get me as soon as he can."

"You sure? Those things take time, you know."

Jennifer looked out the window before answering. The fog had rolled in. Curling over the tiled floor, it reached for the patio chairs with a wet and heavy hand. "I'll wait," she said, a sudden quiet confidence replacing her earlier disappointment. "He'll come back."

IT WAS WAY past midnight when Beck could finally leave. Fleeing the chaos inside the house, he walked to the dusty yard outside the War Wagon and dialed the nursing home's number. The woman on duty told him Jennifer had left hours ago in a cab. He closed his cell phone with a snap and shut his eyes, rubbing his forehead wearily. His headache was almost blinding and had been since he'd walked inside the house. Crossing swords with Randy hadn't helped, either. The sniper had strutted into the death-filled home and made his usual smart-aleck comments. Beck's fist had been drawn back and ready to strike when Lena had walked in unexpectedly.

Something wet and cold touched Beck's fingertips without any warning. His eyes shot open, and he looked down, into the sorrowful gaze of the golden retriever he'd seen earlier. The dog's tail wagged slowly as their eyes connected, then all at once, the animal dropped his head. With a whine more like a sigh, he slouched to the ground, putting his nose on his paws in a gesture of pure dejection.

Beck felt the same way.

He turned and headed for Jennifer's white Toyota, and twenty minutes later, he pulled up outside her condo, remembering her address from Sarah's information. Locating the proper unit, he saw only darkness. She'd probably gone to bed hours before, even more strongly convinced that she wanted nothing to do with him.

He stepped out of the car, exhaustion dragging his steps, and made his way up to the second floor, pausing just outside the door. Nothing but silence and mist surrounded him, the vapor light above the parking lot giving an eerie yellow glow to the fog-shrouded grounds. He wanted to knock on the door, have her open it and pull him inside, into her warmth and understanding and love, but that was a fantasy, and he knew it. His only course of action was to slip her key through her mailbox slot then leave. He started to bend down to do exactly that when he heard a noise from inside. The back light from the peephole went dark, then a second later, the door flew open.

Jennifer stood before him. She had on a long white T-shirt embroidered with little pink hearts. From somewhere behind her, a lamp shone, throwing the light forward to outline her body beneath the cotton.

Beck took what he thought would be a quick look but it lasted a lot longer than he planned. She spoke while his eyes were still on her curves.

"Beck! My God, where have you been? I waited hours at Seacrest for you, but you never came back. I've been so wor—" She broke off at once. Her expression was peeved and her words annoyed, but behind the tension was just what she'd been about to confess to: worry. Her concern, even if she didn't want him to know it, warmed him with a rush of sudden pleasure.

"I had a call," he answered. "I asked the aide—"

"She told me, but—"

"I didn't have the time to find you, Jennifer. I'm sorry, but I had to go and go fast. That's just the way it is."

To cover up her anxiety, she tried to maintain her act, giving her head an impatient toss, her chestnut hair down and full around the curves of her face. It didn't wash with Beck, though. He understood her too well and instead of reacting to her pretense, he found himself responding to the scent of lilacs as it drifted over to where he stood. The fragrance, that sweet, innocent smell, did him in. He grabbed the doorway with his hands in a gesture of absolute weariness and she reached out.

"Are you okay?" she asked softly. Her hands curled around his. "You look like hell."

"That's because I feel like it," he answered. "I

know it's late and I know you're furious with me but can we talk?''

She was immediately torn, indecision battling with her obvious sympathy. She wanted to let him in, but she just wasn't sure. Of herself or of him, he couldn't tell.

''I had a really shitty night.'' He looked directly into her eyes and didn't blink. ''I need a drink…and I need to talk. That's all I want.''

She hesitated for a minute more, then she stepped aside. When he walked into her living room, she spoke from behind him. ''I have some beer. Would that be all right?''

''That would be perfect,'' he answered. Sitting down heavily on her sofa, he closed his eyes, the dreamy image of the watercolor on the opposite wall mixing with the smell of her perfume. Settling into the cushions, he felt something loosen in his chest.

He was almost asleep when she returned a moment later. Opening his eyes, he watched as she set a cold amber bottle on the table beside him. He reached out, circling her wrist with his fingers, and their eyes met again. ''I'm sorry about tonight.''

''I understand,'' she answered. ''I was mad at first, especially after I waited and waited and you didn't come back, but it couldn't be helped, I guess.''

''Believe me, I wish like hell I hadn't gone, but I didn't have a choice. And I'm truly sorry I had to strand you like that. I couldn't take the time to do anything else, though.''

The dark well of her gaze seemed endless. He wanted to fall into it and disappear.

She nodded at his answer. ''Was it bad? What happened, I mean?''

I talked to a dead woman for over an hour. I guess some people might call that bad....

Sensing his hesitation, she spoke. ''If you don't want to tell me...''

''I don't,'' he answered, ''but I need to. Holding this one inside would kill me. I can't do it.''

Taking one step, she started toward the chair near the sofa, but stopped short when he didn't release her wrist.

''Come over here,'' he said. ''Sit by me.''

Without a word, she did as he asked. The cushions moved with her weight when she turned to face him. ''Tell me.'' Her voice was soft and gentle.

''We did everything we could, but it wasn't enough. It was a murder-suicide. A man and his wife.'' He closed his eyes again and described what had happened, leaving out some of the gorier details.

He rubbed his forehead angrily. ''The whole damn thing was so pointless! I talked for two hours and she was already dead—or dying—and I didn't have a clue.'' He turned and met Jennifer's horrified gaze. ''I didn't even know,'' he said hoarsely. ''I didn't know she was there.''

Her eyes welled up and she reached out for him, to bring him to her and give him the comfort he needed so badly. He couldn't have resisted had it cost him his very life, and when he fell into her embrace and buried his face in the sweet curve of her neck, it seemed as if they'd done this very thing a thousand times.

Except for the way his body reacted.

He held her a few seconds more, then he raised his head. Their eyes locked, and he knew he had to kiss her. Nothing else could have possibly happened next. It was ordained. He drew her close and covered her lips with his.

HIS LIPS WERE soft and warm, and Jennifer responded without any thought. She didn't have a choice. Her body took command of her senses and even though she knew she was making a very big mistake, she gave in to the order and kissed Beck back. It didn't matter that he'd stranded her. It didn't matter that she hated his job. It didn't matter that she wanted nothing to do with him.

Nothing mattered but kissing him.

Pressing her mouth against his, she wrapped her arms around his neck and tightened her grip. Beneath her fingers, his blond hair was tangled and damp. He tasted like the fog outside: salty from the sea where it had risen. Feeling her reaction, he pulled her roughly toward him, and deepened his kiss with an almost desperate urgency.

His hands spanned her back and through the thin material of her nightgown, his touch was just as hot and compelling as she'd imagined it would be. Her breasts pressed into his black T-shirt, and through it she caught more of his heat. His body felt as if it were burning from some internal flame.

Her brain tried to intrude, tried to get her to stop, but she ignored the command and continued to kiss him, parting her lips and teasing his tongue with hers. Beck murmured into her open mouth, saying her name over and over, then his lips left hers and trailed down her neck. His beard scratched her, but she didn't care, didn't feel anything but the pleasure building deep inside her.

He brought his hand around and cupped her breast, teasing her nipple until the blazing drive inside her grew even stronger. The feeling shocked her. She couldn't call it desire or even lust. This wasn't anything remotely like those two emotions—it was a genuine need that had to be met regardless of the cost to her heart and soul.

He seemed to experience the same thing at the very same time. Beneath her hands, she felt his body tense, and under her fingers, his muscles grew tight, everything about him turning taut and hard. For a heartbeat longer, he stayed as he was, his mouth on her skin, his hand against her breast, then he tore his lips from her neck and raised his eyes to hers. His gaze was tortured and full of so much pain, she could barely stand to look into the icy blue depths.

"We've got to stop," he said hoarsely. "If we don't, there's no going back."

CHAPTER ELEVEN

HER LIPS WERE FULL and red in the soft light of the lamp, her dark gaze seductive.

"If I carry you into that bedroom behind me and we start to make love, a line gets crossed," he said. "I'm not sure you're ready for that."

"You're not sure *I'm* ready?"

"That's what I said."

"What about you?" she shot back. "Are you ready?"

He searched her eyes. They'd been filled with heat. Now suddenly they were chilly again. He spoke carefully. "You're a beautiful woman, Jennifer. And I want to make love to you."

She blushed, her skin glowing with an apricot tinge. "But…"

"There are no buts," he said. "I want to make love to you, period. When that happens, I don't want you waking up the next morning asking yourself what kind of mistake you've made. And I think you'd do that now. You're not the kind of woman who falls into bed with a guy and doesn't look back."

"How do you know that?"

He didn't answer. All he did was stare at her.

Disentangling herself from his embrace, she stood slowly and walked to the sliding glass door that made up the back wall of her living room. Easing it open, she allowed the night air in, the dampness bringing a chill. The silence built, and Beck didn't know how to break it. Finally, she did it for him.

"You're right." Pivoting, she faced him once more, her arms crossed over her chest, her expression tight. "I *would* feel that way in the morning so maybe you should leave."

He walked to her, and she looked up at him, tilting her neck to frown into his eyes. He couldn't stop himself from reaching out and taking her face between his hands. "When you reach the point where you don't feel that way anymore, I want to know."

"When?" She arched one eyebrow. "Don't you mean *if?"*

He didn't answer right away. Instead, he leaned down and kissed her again, his mouth pressing against hers until she swayed slightly under the onslaught. He'd never tasted a woman so enticing, one who made him want her so much that it hurt. To pull back was torture, but he did, and she blinked as they separated once more.

"I mean when," he answered in a rasping voice. "Otherwise I'd be doomed."

He walked out of her condo and didn't look back. He couldn't. One more glimpse of her half-lidded eyes or swollen mouth and he'd return to pull her into his arms, his pretty little speech nothing but words. He'd been a fool to even go inside in the first place, but he'd felt so completely wiped out, he'd thought it would help him—to see her, to talk to her, to smell her perfume. Instead, those very things had made him realize how much he wanted her. Walking rapidly down the street, he hailed the first cab he saw, and ten minutes later Beck climbed out in front of the station.

When Lena came in at seven the next morning, he was still there. She stared at him in shock, her eyes going over his unshaven face and wrinkled clothes. "Beck! What on earth are you doing here? Didn't you go home last night?"

"No." He concentrated on the paperwork in front of him. His vision was fuzzy, and his mouth tasted like something from the sewer, probably because of the motor oil-like coffee he'd been swigging all night. Taking another sip from the mug in front of him, he scribbled something on the form he was filling out. "I didn't go home last night. I went to Jennifer's. And then I came here. What's your problem with that?"

She blinked at his brusqueness but her gaze went steely, and she sat down in the chair beside his desk, dropping her briefcase on the floor by her feet. "I don't have a problem with you seeing Jennifer Barclay. I might wonder how it affects your ability to deal with the incident, but you seem to have moved on so I guess it's not an issue. My problem with you is your inability to judge your own readiness. What if the phone rang right now and we caught a call? Could you go out and be effective? I don't think so."

"I'd be as effective right now as I was last night," he answered bitterly. "What difference would it make?"

She stared at him for a minute, then pursed her lips. "That's it," she said. "You're going on vacation. Right now."

"I can't—"

"Don't even try," she said, interrupting him. "There's nothing you can say that will change my mind. I want you out of here. And that's an order."

Beck's hands went into fists. "You don't understand—"

"Oh, really? What part don't I understand? The part where you're exhausted and don't even know it? Or the part where you've lost all patience with Randy and have no tolerance around him? Maybe you mean the part where you're feeling sorry for yourself because of last night? Which one is it, Beck? Tell me."

He stared at her through bleary eyes.

She rose and grabbed her briefcase. "Get out, Beck. And I don't mean out of the station. I want you to leave town. For at least a week. You need a change of scenery."

"No." He stood as well. Towering over her, he shook his head stubbornly. "I'm not leaving town."

They glared at each other, a standoff in the making.

"And your reason is...?" she demanded.

His brain felt as unclear as his eyesight; he was exhausted and dispirited, but he knew one thing. He didn't want to abandon Jennifer. When she'd told him about her meeting with Maria, he'd felt a surge of protectiveness that surprised him. Now, with the memory of the kiss they'd shared still burning in his mind and the way she'd defended him to Nancy Thomas still ringing in his ears, he felt an even stronger bond. He didn't want to leave town, or her, for an hour, much less a week.

"Why isn't important," he answered. He crossed his arms. "I'll go home, but I'm staying here in Destin. And not for a week, either. Three days. That's it."

Lena stared at him with incredulous eyes. "This isn't a standoff, Beck! You don't have a choice so don't try that negotiating shit with me!"

He started to argue, to offer an alternative plan, then he thought about it. Lena *was* his boss; whatever she said, he needed to do. But he couldn't. It was just that simple.

He made his expression contrite and held up his hands in a sign of defeat. "You're absolutely right, Lena. I'm sorry. I'll do it. I'll get my crap and go to the house right now and pack. I'll take off in the morning...." Turning to his desk, he began to shuffle the papers strewn across its scarred wooden surface.

She watched him go through the motions, then after a minute, she put her hand on his arm, as he'd known she would. He raised his face wearing what he hoped was an innocent expression.

"Beck, look, just get out of the station, okay? If you don't want to take a trip, I understand. But you need a break. We all do after last night, but you most of all. You're losing your perspective."

He'd gotten what he wanted, but he didn't like her tone. "What do you mean?"

"That fight with Randy—it was pointless. I know there's a problem with him, he's wild and uncontrollable. You've made me aware of it, but decking him wouldn't have helped, and you would know that if you had some balance in your life."

He clenched his jaw. "The guy's not a team player, Lena. What does he have to do before you see that?"

"We're discussing *your* problems here, Beck. Not Randy's." She frowned at him with an unflinching expression. "You got me to do exactly what you planned. Go home. But don't come back for a week."

THE BEACH WAS lonely and deserted. Snowy white sand stretched for miles in either direction and as far as Jennifer could see, the expanse was empty. Everyone had departed an hour ago leaving her behind with her thoughts, but, earlier, she and three parents had supervised more than a dozen kids. They'd spent the whole day, running up and down the water's edge, picking up trash and looking for shells. The annual cleanup was really an excuse to give the students some fun time; Destin kept its beaches pristine. There was rarely any kind of debris to be seen, other than an occasional drink can or the scattered flotsam dumped from a ship cruising near shore.

That was one of the reasons Jennifer loved the area. Always clean, always uncluttered, the beaches and clear green water offered the exact parallel to what she sought in her life. Until now.

Her feet sinking into the clingy sand, she stared at the horizon and wondered what was happening to her. Beck's kiss had turned her upside down and inside out. She'd had her share of lovers, some better than others, but she'd never been kissed like that before. His mouth had molded to hers as if they'd been made for each other, the fit so perfect and right, she'd been astonished. That wasn't what had stolen her breath and stopped her heart, however. No, what had done that was him pulling back when she hadn't been able to do so herself.

Had he known? Could he tell? His words rang in her mind. *When you reach the point where you don't feel that way anymore, I want to know.*

Shading her eyes with her hand, she looked into the brilliant sunset that hovered over the water, the streaks of purple, gold and red etching their way into her mind as sharply as the emotions that had attacked her when he'd spoken. Disappointment. Frustration. Acceptance.

He was right, of course. If they'd made love, she *would* have chastised herself later. They'd only known each other three weeks! She *didn't* sleep with strangers. It was not only dangerous, it just didn't feel right. She wanted love and a family, a white picket fence and a secure little life. All the things she'd not had as a child…and all the things Beck couldn't give her, either.

An unexpected memory rose to the forefront of her thoughts. Her father's birthday was coming up and he'd called the night before. He'd been out for more than a month and when the phone rang late that night, her mother had gone rigid in her chair. She'd looked at Jennifer with alarm and told her to answer it. Her own heart kicking up a notch, Jennifer had barely been able to hear him, the line scratchy and filled with echoes. She'd handed the receiver to her mother, and she'd begun to speak to him, her face wreathed in a smile Jennifer simply didn't understand. After she'd hung up, she'd said "Your daddy's coming home tomorrow. We'll bake him a chocolate cake and decorate it to surprise him."

The next morning, they'd driven to the PX and bought the special kind of bitter chocolate he liked, then spent the rest of the day on the elaborate confection. It'd been hot and sticky, Jennifer remembered, the windows of their small on-base bungalow open wide to catch what little cool air they could, the Gulf Coast humidity making their clothes cling and their hair curl.

Then they'd waited. And waited. And waited some more. A week later, her mother had thrown the cake in the trash can, untouched.

Four days after that, he'd called and said "something had happened." Jennifer never forgot the look on her mother's face. A curtain of disappointment and hurt came over her that didn't leave for a long time, even after he returned.

Wasn't something like that ahead for any woman who fell in love with Beck? He wasn't her father, of course, yet Beck's life was worlds away from what she really wanted. Where was the cottage, the kids, the station wagon?

But his lips... They'd felt so good! And his hands... She closed her eyes briefly and considered what they could do to her. After a quick, forbidden image, she put the idea aside. She couldn't even begin to imagine what making love with him would feel like.

She shook herself mentally, her feet taking her farther down the beach, the clear, warm water lapping at her toes. She'd just felt sorry for him, that's all. He'd had an unbelievably bad night and she'd let her sympathy get the better of her. The agonized look in his eyes, the guilt he'd taken on—anyone would have responded as she did. She'd only wanted to comfort him and she'd done it the best way she knew how.

"Who are you trying to kid?" she said out loud to a seagull strutting nearby. "Comfort him? What a crock!"

The bird bobbed his head up and down, his white-and-grey feathers ruffling in the evening breeze as he let out a loud squawk. He agreed with her, obviously. She was a fool and an idiot; a fool for thinking more about the kiss and an idiot for hoping her life would stay unchanged should she get involved with Beck.

She watched the sun ease closer to the shoreline, the last crimson rays tinting the surf with gold, then she made a wide arc in the sand, heading back to where she'd started. She'd grab a pizza, go home and watch a movie. That's what she usually did on Thursday night, and that's what she'd do tonight. She had to put Beck and his kiss behind her. They had no future together, and it was time she quit acting silly and accepted that. The thought calmed her and as she walked down the hard-packed beach, she knew she was making the right decision. She *had* to get her life on track. That was the only thing she could depend on.

She reached the wooden stairs linking the shore to the parking lot a few minutes later. In the evening breeze, the tall grasses beneath the open steps whispered and swayed among the dunes. She breathed deeply of their calm, soothing scent, then she picked up the tennis shoes she'd left by the bottom stair and grabbed the handrail. She felt better now that her decision was made.

Then she started up the stairs. Beck met her halfway down.

JENNIFER'S FACE was shadowed as she stared up at him, but he could tell she was surprised to see him by the way she spoke. "Beck! What are you doing here?"

He stopped as he reached the stair where she stood. "I'm not stalking you, I promise. I knew about the cleanup and hoped you'd still be here." He took a deep breath and met her puzzled stare. "I came to apologize, Jennifer. I've been told I'm losing my perspective and after I thought about it a bit, I decided that might be right. So I'm sorry I showed up at your house at midnight and I'm sorry for everything else. Can you forgive me?"

"There's nothing to forgive. I should have understood the situation better, anyway." She smiled, but then her expression faded and filled with concern. "What's wrong, Beck? You look as if you just lost your best friend."

He lifted his head and stared out the water. He couldn't remember the last time he'd been to the beach and the gentle call of the surf lured him closer. "Come walk with me, and I'll tell you."

She thought about it for a moment, then she answered quickly, as if she were afraid she might try to change her own mind. "All right."

Beck took her hand in his and they started down the sand. Ten full minutes passed before he began to speak. Anyone else would have wanted to break the quiet, but not Jennifer, he noticed. She was comfortable with silence.

"Lena kicked me out," he said. "She told me to take a week off and not come back to the station for a while."

Jennifer's eyebrows lifted. "Oh, my gosh! Why?"

"She thinks I need a vacation."

"Do you?"

There was barely enough light to see her eyes now, but he could hear the compassion in her voice. "Yeah," he answered, "I think I do, but I don't want to."

"You don't want to go or you don't want to need one?"

"Both," he said slowly. "I can't stand the idea of 'needing' time off—"

"But, Beck, everyone requires a break now and then. And with your work…"

He nodded. "I know, I know. And I've actually made guys on my team do the same thing, but it didn't feel right when Lena told me I had to. But besides that, I don't want to leave town."

"Why not?"

He stopped and turned to meet her eyes. They were

still holding hands, and as he looked at her, he covered her fingers with all of his. "I don't want to leave you."

"I—I don't understand...." The words were spoken, but her gaze, still on his, said something entirely different.

She wasn't ready to acknowledge their growing closeness.

"I'm not sure I do, either," he answered, going along with her. "But it's the way I feel."

The waves rushed along the shore beside them, the growing darkness surrounding them. She said nothing.

"Look, Jennifer, I've gone through some of the same things you're experiencing—the nightmares, the flashbacks, the anger—and it's not good stuff, especially if you're alone. I want to be here for you."

"You can't stop them—"

"I know." He tightened his grip and gently squeezed her hand. "But I want to be here in case you need me. It's just how I feel so don't ask me to change my mind."

"And if you're wrong?"

"It wouldn't be the first time. I'd live."

She didn't answer. She simply stared at him, and a moment later, they started walking again, the white, powdery sand slipping beneath their feet. They seemed to cross an invisible bridge. Ten yards down the beach, he spoke again. "Tell me about your brother."

"I don't think—"

"Just tell me," he said, looking off toward the horizon. "I want to hear the story."

They walked a few more yards, the sandpipers scurrying ahead of them, skipping over the waves and pecking at the sand in search of food.

"I was ten when he died," she said slowly. "I saw it happen."

"Damn. That must have been tough."

She nodded. "Seeing someone die is not something you forget...but I guess you know that."

"It's never easy, but it's different if you love the person."

She stayed silent for a few seconds, then began to speak again. "We were living at Hulbert Field, in Fort Walton, and my father had just returned from a four-month mission. We had no idea where he'd been, as always. While he'd been gone, though, my brother turned sixteen, and he'd been making some of the decisions around the house...stuff my mom would ask him about." She shook her head. "None of the problems were earth-shattering. I think she mainly asked his help to boost his self-confidence."

"Did it work?"

"Oh, yes. He seemed really happy there for a while. Then Dad came home."

"What happened?"

She kicked at the surf as a wave came close. Her toenails were painted pink. "Dad did his usual thing. Started taunting him, teasing him, calling him names. Said Danny wasn't a real man and he was kidding himself if he thought he was." Looking out over the water, her gaze didn't see the sunset, he was sure.

"He took us to the training field one afternoon. You know, where they do the running and the tower climbing...all the stuff the new recruits have to go through. I could scamper through it like a monkey. I loved sports and did well at almost all of them. Danny was just the opposite. He was artistic. He didn't have a shred of athletic ability, but he loved to draw and paint. He did fantastic watercolors. I have one hanging on the wall opposite my couch."

Beck nodded. "I saw it."

She smiled sadly. "He wasn't yet fifteen when he painted that. He was so very talented...but it ended that day. Dad teased him unmercifully." She deepened her voice. "'You think you're a man? Shit, boy, you don't even know the meaning of the word. Your sister can climb that pole a hundred times faster and she's just a ten-year-old girl! Don't even try 'cause you won't make it.'

"Danny took the bait, of course. I knew I should try to stop him, but I was afraid of Dad, too, and Danny was determined to make Dad shut up once and for all." Her voice wavered just a bit. "It was hotter than hell and he was wearing an old Rolling Stones

T-shirt. He'd sweated completely through it. He looked over at me, then walked to the pole and started to climb.''

She took a deep breath, held it then let it out slowly. "He did pretty good at first. He made it past halfway, almost to the top. Then he looked down."

Her tone became matter-of-fact. "He fell fifteen feet and broke his neck. He landed right beside me."

Beck felt himself flinch inwardly. The pain she was hiding behind her attitude was just as fresh and raw as it had been back then. "God, Jennifer..."

She acknowledged his sympathy with a nod. "It was terrible. My mother was completely wiped out. I think she started down the path to where she is right now because of it. She has more than just Alzheimer's. It's complicated so I generally don't explain everything."

"And you?"

"I blamed my father." She glanced up. "And I still do. Danny would never have died if it hadn't been for him."

They walked farther down the beach, the salt spray stinging their faces, the wind picking up. No wonder she wanted her life to be calm and peaceful. She linked everything bad that had happened to her to her father and his job. There was more to it than that, though. She blamed herself just as much.

Guilt. It was a powerful emotion and Beck understood that fact intimately. It motivated him, too.

She spoke after a while. "I've told you all my secrets. Now it's your turn. Tell me about your ex-wife."

The question surprised him, and he felt a spurt of hope because she cared enough to ask. He told himself he was acting stupid, but the feeling remained.

"It was not a match made in heaven," he answered after a few steps. "Dixie had her share of quirks and I had mine. They weren't the same and didn't quite mesh."

"But you loved her once?"

"Of course," he answered. "Desperately. Then I figured out why and it scared the hell out of me."

She looked up and raised an eyebrow, the unvoiced question obvious.

"I rescued her," he said. "She was a hooker, working Front Street, and I felt sorry for her. I married her to get her out of the life, then it went to hell pretty fast after that. We had nothing in common."

They'd covered a few more yards as he'd spoken, but Jennifer stopped as he finished speaking. She didn't appear shocked by his revelation about Dixie, but she didn't look happy, either.

"Is that what's going on here?" Her face glowed in the aftermath of the last ray of sun. Beside them, the surf picked up its pace, the foamy waves coming in a little faster. "Are you rescuing me? Because if you are, we'd better quit this right now. I don't need someone to take care of me."

She was so beautiful, he felt his gut tighten. "Are you sure?"

Her eyes flared. "Of course, I'm sure. I've been on my—"

"On your own for years, I know. And so have I," he answered. "But I'd still like someone to meet me at the door and kiss me hello." He paused and held back the urge to gather her into his arms. "We all need to be rescued one way or the other, Jennifer. That's just part of life."

BY THE TIME they made their way back to their parked cars, Jennifer didn't know what to think. Her heart was in more turmoil than it had been a few days before. Something about Beck was drawing her closer and closer, and it scared her so much, she didn't know what to do. She was fighting the attraction, but it was a losing battle, and she knew it.

They stopped beside the cars. Jennifer's back was to the Toyota's door and Beck stood before her, his arms on either side of her shoulders, trapping her as she leaned against the automobile. They were surrounded by the isolation, the old beach road empty this late in the day. Beyond the dunes, the waves had begun to rise with the late tide, their noisy arrival filling the empty silence.

She knew he was going to kiss her again. She could tell by the way he was looking at her. His eyes were hungry, and with a start, she realized her own probably held the same kind of need. She put her hands on his chest and started to stop him, but she was too late, and he told her so.

"It's pointless," he said. "Don't even try to tell me it's not going to happen."

She shook her head. "Beck—"

He lowered his head, talking to her as he did so, his breath warm and tantalizing. "I'm going to kiss you, Jennifer. And you're going to kiss me back."

He pressed his mouth against hers and she gave in to the sensation of the kiss, of the touch, of the smell. She wanted him so badly, she couldn't even fight it. What she had told him was certainly true; she didn't need rescuing, but right now, she definitely needed this kiss. Her mouth opened to his and he slid his tongue inside, gently insistent, his hands tightening on her back.

With the empty sky overhead and the velvet night enveloping them, Jennifer felt her world tilt and slide. There was nothing to hang on to except Beck, and she clutched his shirt, his muscular back hard and tight beneath her fingers. The heat of his body traveled the full length of hers, the obvious strength of his desire making itself known. He groaned and whispered her name.

The kiss went on until Jennifer pulled back, her heart thumping so hard against her ribs it was almost as loud as the roar of the surf behind them. "I—I don't think this would please the school board," she said breathlessly. "I can see the headlines now. Schoolteacher Caught Making Out With Cop At Local Beach. Betty already thinks I'm a nutcase. This would seal the deal for sure."

"Do you really care what she thinks?"

His eyes were bright, even in the darkness.

Jennifer met their stark expression and slowly shook her head. "No…I don't actually think I do now that you ask."

"Then kiss me again." His voice was a low rumble and where it touched her skin, it lingered. "Make me think you really mean that."

Nodding slowly, she fell into his gaze, then she did what he wanted. She moved closer and tangled her hands behind his neck. A second later, she kissed him again.

CHAPTER TWELVE

JENNIFER DIDN'T KNOW how it happened, but Beck drove off smiling. Somehow, he'd managed to get her to agree to dinner the following Saturday. She told herself over and over that it was just a meal, nothing more, but by Wednesday, she was a nervous wreck. That evening, she visited the nursing home, as usual, and had a long conversation with her mother. Actually, Nadine sat by blankly while Jennifer talked, only it didn't seem to help.

Her students added to the confusion, too. They were absolutely wild as the school year drew to a close. On Thursday, the last day of classes, everything was chaos. Jennifer spent most of the day having fun with the kids. The nightmare they'd been through seemed far behind them until Juan approached Jennifer late that afternoon. He was hiding something behind his back but as he drew close he brought his hands around with a shy look and held out a carefully wrapped package to her.

"It's from my *mamá*." His voice was so low she could barely hear it.

"Oh, Juan!" A lot of the children brought her presents at the end of the year, but this one represented a real sacrifice. The family had so little. "This truly wasn't necessary."

"Yes, it is." His expression reflected his seriousness. "Open it and I will explain."

She did as he directed, slowly undoing the ribbon and peeling back the tissue paper both of which had been folded precisely. The small white box was heavy.

Nestled inside on a bed of cotton a silver cross winked up at her. Six inches long and maybe three inches across, its gleaming surface was decorated with small symbols, also made of silver. Jennifer didn't know what they meant, but she recognized the value of the piece immediately. What had the Canaleses done without to buy her this? Her eyes filled with tears.

"Oh my, Juan! This is so beautiful!" She reached out without thinking and wrapped her arms around the little boy.

He responded by putting his own around her neck then dropped them quickly, clearly embarrassed. "I-it's a *milagro*," he stammered to cover up his chagrin.

Jennifer knew enough Spanish to recognize the word. "A miracle?"

He nodded. "My family knows a miracle took place the day Mr. French came into our classroom. You covered me up after the shooting began. You saved my life. My *mamá* wanted to give you this.

The symbols on the cross represent different parts of your body. It will keep you safe and healthy, too.''

A lump came into Jennifer's throat. ''I don't know what to say, Juan. You're the one who was brave that day, not me.''

''No, no. I wasn't brave.'' He shook his head. ''I was scared.''

Their eyes met over the shining silver. ''So was I,'' she said. ''So was I.''

Jennifer felt her vision blur again then she reached out once more and hugged him tightly. A second later, he ran off and joined the other children.

At 7:00 p.m. Saturday, she was standing nervously on her balcony, trying to calm herself with a glass of white wine. The minute she saw Beck's truck pull into the parking lot, she grabbed her purse and shawl and ran out the front door, throwing the lock behind her. If he came up those stairs and they started kissing, she was afraid they wouldn't even make it to dinner and that wasn't what she wanted to happen. Or so she told herself.

They met on the sidewalk downstairs. Beck's slow perusal of her sleeveless knit sheath made her wish she'd picked something less attractive. His eyes burned through the fabric and touched her body so intimately it felt as though she'd left the dress off completely.

''Very nice,'' he said slowly. ''You look good in

black…but then I haven't seen you look bad in anything yet.''

Heat suffused her body and made its way to her face. His compliment was nice, but in reality the praise should have been going in the opposite direction. With his navy herringbone slacks and a collarless white shirt, he looked so downright sexy, she was twice as glad she'd met him downstairs. His blond hair was slicked back, but one strand fell down over his forehead. The almost white shade of the curl made his tan seem even darker, but as always, his eyes were what captured her attention. Their intensity pulled her gaze like a flame she couldn't avoid, even though she knew it'd burn her.

He led her down to his truck and helped her climb inside. She was in such a fog she didn't even know what their small talk covered, but twenty minutes later, they pulled up in front of the Marina Café. Following the tall redhead who led them through the elegant restaurant, Jennifer felt beautiful and alluring and desirable and she knew exactly why. It was because of Beck. Every woman in the restaurant stopped and stared at him. His presence and aura of sexuality made it impossible for them to do anything else.

They took a table near the back, beside a bank of windows that looked out over the harbor. The slips were lined up outside the glass, just off the deck, so close Jennifer felt she could reach out and touch them. Every spot held a boat, some small, some big, but all impressive, their paint gleaming in the late-evening sun, the water lapping at their sleek white hulls. Tall, weathered pilings divided the openings, and on top of almost every pole sat a huge, grey pelican.

As soon as they were settled, the waiter appeared and took their drink orders. Beck looked over at her and smiled. "Thank you for coming with me tonight. I guess my powers of persuasion haven't completely failed me."

"I don't think they'd ever do that." She played nervously with the napkin beside her plate. "Your arguments are hard to resist."

He reached across the table and took her hand in his, stilling her fingers. "I'm glad to hear that. But not everyone agrees, you know."

"You mean the criminals you arrest after they give up?"

"Yeah. They usually aren't too thrilled with the situation. Sometimes they blame me." He shrugged. "That's the way it goes, though. As long as they don't come out shooting, I don't mind."

Her throat started to tighten, but she forced herself to relax. "Does that happen often?"

"Me getting shot at?"

She nodded tersely.

"Actually, no. We've caught some pretty bad situations lately, but a vast majority of the time, SWAT calls are answered and resolved without any shots exchanged. You just don't hear about it. The TV cameras show the bloody, disastrous ones instead. Ratings, I guess.''

Jennifer shivered lightly. ''I don't understand. Why would someone want to watch stuff like that?''

''Because they've never experienced it,'' he answered in a matter-of-fact way. ''They think of it as entertainment. They don't appreciate that they're seeing real people get hurt. To them, it's just happening on the screen and nowhere else.''

She met his gaze over the flickering candle that sat on the table. ''But it *is* real. Howard French was a person who lived and died. *I'm* real. And my, God, the children, they're real.''

''You're preaching to the choir.'' His jaw went tight, and she could hear the emotion behind his words. ''I know all that.''

She forced herself to pull back and relax. They were here for dinner, nothing more. They didn't have to solve the problems of the world. Beck seemed to think the same thing at the same time, and when the waiter brought their drinks then left, he raised his glass to hers and tapped the rim. ''To a nice dinner and good friends,'' he said with a smile. *''Salut.''*

The crystal rims rang as she brought her drink to his. They drank in silence then watched an immaculate yacht glide through the harbor waters.

''I wouldn't mind having a boat like that some day,'' Beck said thoughtfully. ''Stand at the wheel, sail around the world, forget about everything…''

She looked across the white tablecloth in surprise. This was a side of him she'd never seen before. Where was the driven, focused cop? "You'd quit the force?"

He waited a second before answering. "If you'd asked me that five years ago, I would have said no way. Now, I'm not so sure."

Intrigued, she leaned closer, resting her chin in the cup of her hand. "Why is that? What made you change your mind?"

"Well, at first, you're in love with the idea of being a cop. You have to be, otherwise, you wouldn't make it. Getting into a police academy isn't easy—only about two out of every one hundred applicants make it. For a SWAT team, it's tougher." His gaze went down to his drink. "After you're accepted and actually going through the training, all you can do is worry about finishing it. You only have time for studying and pleasing the FTO—the field training officer. If you're lucky enough to pass, then the good part comes."

"And that is?"

"The job. It's great. You try to improve all the time, you think you're helping folks, you bend over backward to do things by the book and live right. Every day's a challenge. Nothing matters but the job." He took a sip of his drink and met her look. "That's when I got married, and it was the worst possible time."

"The worst time? But I'd think—"

"I know, I know. That's what I thought, too. That it'd be the best, but I was gone all hours of the night and day, and Dixie hated it. We fought over my time away and then we didn't even fight. She just left. After that, things shifted for me."

"What do you mean?"

"I started wondering if I was doing the right thing. That's when I wanted to quit but went into SWAT, instead. I enjoyed it a lot until I saw how wrong it could go, how totally screwed up the runs could get, even more so than on the regular squad." He shook his head. "The potential for disaster is always greater with a specialized team. Bad things happen. Really bad things. That's why the members are so important."

Something in his voice clued her in, and the hair rose on the back of her neck. She tensed. "Like people getting killed?"

"Yes," he said evenly. "Like people getting killed."

She wanted to press him. Was he thinking of Howard or the time he'd mentioned before when he'd gone into therapy with Maria? Jennifer started to ask, but at that very second, the waiter reappeared. "May I tell you about our specials this evening?"

After the man left, the moment was gone. Beck seemed to sense what she was about to ask, and he took the conversation in a different direction. She thought of returning to the issue, but what was the point? She told herself it didn't matter, and the rest of the meal, they chatted about inconsequential things. By the time dessert was served, Jennifer found herself relaxing once more. Beck was an easy person to talk to, entertaining and complex. Unlike a lot of men she'd gone out with, he didn't talk just about himself. They discussed the state of the world, religion and money. It was remarkable how much they agreed on.

The arrival of a large party, noisy and bent on celebrating, brought their conversation to a temporary halt. She and Beck watched as a dozen or so people circled around a nearby table. They'd brought balloons and flowers and everything else they needed to commemorate the birthday of their matriarch. The obviously pleased gray-haired woman walked slowly down the aisle toward them, and Jennifer felt a flash of sorrow. She would have liked to do that sort of thing for her own mother, but the noise and people and confusion would never have worked for Nadine. Instead of being happy, she would have been scared.

One of the younger members of the party, undoubtedly a grandchild, ran up to the older woman and pulled out her chair. Dark-haired with flashing eyes and a quick smile, the little boy was precious, dressed to the nines in a suit and so delighted to be helping his grandmother that he could hardly stand still. His exuberance and shining black hair immediately brought Juan to her mind. Jennifer smiled then caught Beck's eye, the thought flashing into her head that he'd make a terrific father.

And that's when it happened.

The child yanked on the red balloon they'd tied to the grandmother's chair. The bright sphere dipped, then unexpectedly popped.

Jennifer's vision tunneled without any warning. The harbor, the restaurant, even Beck's face grew small then disappeared. She knew what was going on, but there was nothing she could do to stop it. The progression was inevitable. Fighting a swamping wave of dizziness, she tried anyway and pushed back from the table, rising unsteadily to her feet.

The movement only made things worse.

Gripping the edge of the table, Jennifer swayed, and everything else—all the rest of her senses— started to fade. The only remaining sensation she had was a flash of heat that rolled over her, starting at the top of her head and streaking its way to her feet. It felt as if a flame was rippling down her. She broke into a sweat, but strangely she shivered.

A moment later, Beck's blue gaze, full of alarm and shock, came into focus then disappeared for good. The next thing she saw was Howard's terrified face, then a mist of red. The foglike cloud spread into a fine rain and hit her, the drops staining her dress and face with crimson. She tried to brush it off, but the damning evidence coated her hands and refused to leave.

She stared at her fingertips, then moaned and crumpled to the floor.

THE WHOLE THING took only a second. Beck understood the look on Jennifer's face even before she knew what was occurring, but he was still too late. Throwing his chair behind him, he jumped up and ran to her side of the table where he knelt down beside her.

She was out cold. He swept her into his arms, then strode quickly to the rear of the restaurant with her limp and almost weightless body in his embrace. A private dining room spanned the whole back area. They disappeared into the empty area so fast he was sure only the waiter actually saw what happened. He took one look, then ran toward the front of the restaurant.

The redhead who'd led Beck and Jennifer to their table earlier in the evening appeared a few moments after that. There was concern in her voice. "Is she all right? Can I do anything?"

"She'll be fine," Beck said. "Bring me a wet towel and some ice. Some brandy, too."

The woman hurried away and Beck gently placed Jennifer on the carpeted floor, pulling a cushion from a nearby chair to put under her neck. Her face was ghostly, her lipsticked mouth a slash of dark pink against the ivory skin. Beneath the thin lids of her eyes, he could see movement, rapid and anxious. Her breathing was shallow as well, her chest rising and falling far too swiftly. She moaned and turned her head against the damask seat cushion.

"It's okay," he whispered. "It's okay, Jennifer."

The hostess appeared a moment later and handed Beck what he'd needed. With quick, efficient movements, he bathed Jennifer's face, then wrapped the towel around some of the ice and put it behind her neck.

"Do you want me to call an ambulance?" the woman asked.

"No, no." Beck didn't look up. "That's not necessary. She's okay, just give us a bit of time here."

"Of course, take all you need. And please call us if we can do anything else."

He heard her move away and then they were alone again.

"Jennifer? Jennifer, can you hear me?" He took another ice cube from the bowl and eased it over Jennifer's forehead.

She groaned and her eyelids fluttered.

"C'mon now. Wake up. It's time to come back."

Slowly she opened her eyes. Her gaze was still unfocused and vague, but as he watched, she became more aware and remembrance filled her expression. As if yanked by a string, she sat up abruptly, her eyes wild and frightened as she reached out for him, her chest heaving with alarm. "Beck!"

He put his arms around her. "It's okay, honey. It's okay." Rubbing her back with wide circles, he tried to calm her trembling. "Slow down. Breathe. You're all right."

She continued to shake in his embrace, then all at once she started to sway again, even though she was sitting. He pulled back and lowered her head to her knees, his hand on the back of her neck. "Breathe in," he commanded. "Breathe!"

In a moment, he felt her spine expand. "Let it out slowly." She followed his orders. "Once more," he said. After three more deep breaths, she lifted her head and stared at him. Her skin still looked clammy, but two spots of color now dotted her cheeks.

"My God..." She shook her head slowly. "Wh-what happened?"

"A balloon popped. Do you remember?"

"No." She spoke slowly, a dazed look on her face as she brought her hand to her hair and pushed it back off her forehead. "I don't. I remember we were eating and talking and then..."

"The family came in," he prompted.

She stared at him, her eyes narrowing in concentration. "A family?"

He nodded. "Lots of people with an older woman. A little boy ran up..."

Her hand went to her throat. "Oh, my God, I remember now. He reminded me of Juan, and then the sound. It scared me…the noise of the balloon. I heard it, and then all of a sudden—'' She broke off and stared at him, her mouth falling open.

''You had a flashback.''

She nodded and began to cry softly as he put his arms around her once more. ''I—I saw Howard,'' she whispered against his neck. ''It was h-horrible. There was blood and it wouldn't come off me….''

''Shhh. Shhh…'' He held on tight, her body trembling against his, her tears staining his shirt. ''I'm here. It's okay.''

She hiccuped into silence and Beck rocked back on his heels to reach behind him, one arm still around her. He gave her the glass of brandy. ''Drink this.''

She lifted the crystal tumbler in hands that were still unsteady. Two sips later she grimaced and set it down. ''I can't believe this happened. I felt badly that day at the grocery store, but it was nothing compared to this. God, I feel so foolish.''

''Don't.'' He stared at her with a frown. ''It's perfectly understandable for someone who went through what you did. Didn't Maria tell you that?''

''Yes, but—''

''Yes, but, nothing. You didn't do anything wrong.''

She nodded, then took another sip of brandy. When she raised her gaze to his, her brown eyes were full of tears. "Beck, can you hold me again? Just a little while longer?"

He smiled gently and opened his arms. "Actually, yes, I think I can arrange to do just that."

DESPITE WHAT Beck had said, Jennifer still felt foolish. While he paid their bill, she waited for him outside, on the walkway by the marina, and cringed as she remembered more of the incident. What had everyone in the elegant restaurant thought when she'd cried out then collapsed? She couldn't imagine.

The door opened and Beck walked out. Coming toward her, he smiled reassuringly. "You doing okay?"

"I'm a little shaky but I'll make it."

He nodded. "Let's walk to the end of the dock and get you some sea air."

They headed toward the pilings that marked the end of the pier. On either side of them, water slapped the hulls of the boats with an almost hypnotic rhythm. Jennifer took a deep breath. The salty air did feel good as it entered her lungs, clear and sharp.

He kept the conversation light—just what she needed—until they reached the railing that stopped their progress. Looking down at the water, Jennifer shook her head. "I'm so sorry, Beck. Did I...did I embarrass you back there?"

He laughed deeply, the sound echoing over the calm dark water that stretched before them. "Jennifer! C'mon, I'm a cop. You could take off all your clothes and dance a jig and I wouldn't be embarrassed. Hell, there's nothing you can do or say I haven't seen before.''

She laughed, too. "Well, that may be true, but I'm sure most of your dates don't end that way. With the woman screaming then fainting.''

He leaned one elbow against the railing then reached out with his other hand and trailed a finger down her arm. She tried not to shiver. "Sure they do," he said easily. "But it usually happens later...in my bedroom.''

He grinned then, and she couldn't help but return the expression, his humor relaxing her and making the moment less awkward.

Slowly he leaned toward her. "It's all right," he said. "I've been there myself.''

"Will it end?''

"Yes, it will," he answered. "If you stick with Maria and work through the problem. If you push the memories deeper and try to ignore them, then no.'' A silver-white sailboat glided by in ghostly silence, the water's surface barely broken by its passage. "I've tried it both ways so I know.''

Jennifer couldn't help herself. She lifted her hand to his face and gently traced the line of his jaw with her finger. "Tell me what happened to you," she said softly. "I need to know.''

He captured her fingers and brought them to his

lips. For a long moment, he held her hand there, his mouth warming her skin. When he released her, it was only so he could pull her into his arms. Looking down at her with his pale, blue glaze, he stared for a second, then closed his eyes. "I went into a house with three other cops. I had the lead. We were trying to serve a high-risk arrest warrant on a repeat sexual offender. That's all we knew." He swallowed. "He wasn't supposed to be violent and Intelligence had told us he had no arms, no weapons...but they were wrong. He had a modified Uzi and he opened it up the minute we broke in. Somehow—God only knows how—he missed me and got the rest of the team. Every one of them. Then he turned around and shot the four kids he'd lured into his living room."

"Oh, my God." He'd told the story without any emotion, in a cold, hard way almost as if he were reading it from a script. The realization came to her that this was probably the only way he *could* recount what had happened, and her heart broke as if he'd cried instead. She asked the question gently. "Did you arrest him—"

"I shot him." His jaw clenched. "I wish he could have died more than once."

He met her eyes. The look that passed between them was quick, but the feeling it created was so strong it stole her pulse. They were different in so many ways she couldn't count them, but they were alike, too. They shared too much to ignore and she was a fool for thinking he was like her father. Beck was nothing like the man she'd grown up avoiding. She raised her hands and pulled Beck's face down to hers. The kiss was long and deep and said everything she didn't have the words for. When they broke apart, he spoke in a husky voice.

"Come home with me."

She looked into his blue eyes and nodded once.

BECK PUT THE KEY into the lock of his apartment door and turned it slowly, his eyes on Jennifer's face. She was still pale, still shaky, but she'd seemed determined enough when he'd asked her to return home with him. Now, he wasn't so sure. She tugged nervously at the gold necklace around her neck and spoke.

"So this is it, huh?"

Without speaking, he nodded and pushed the door open. She preceded him into the entry, her high heels tapping on the tile foyer until she stopped at the edge of the carpet that marked the living room's boundary. "How long have you lived here?"

He took her shawl from her outstretched hand and draped it over a nearby bar stool. "A few years," he answered. "It's close to the station, and the beach, too."

"It looks new." She turned. "No pictures on the walls? No plants? No dog?"

"I'm not a very responsible person. I'd kill a plant

and probably starve a dog.'' He shrugged. ''My hours are a good excuse for a lot of things.'' He put his hands on her shoulders and looked down into her eyes. In the single lamp's light, they were huge and soulful. ''I didn't bring you here to tell you all my shortcomings,'' he said. ''I had something else in mind….''

Her tongue slipped out and moistened her lips. ''I know that.''

She looked so impossibly kissable Beck didn't bother to try to resist. He lowered his head to hers and proceeded to kiss her. With a tiny, almost imperceptible moan, she responded, her breath as sweet and heady as the brandy she'd sipped earlier.

Drawing her close, Beck moved his hands to her shoulders then down, following the curve of her spine with his fingers. Her dress went into a V between her shoulders and he let his touch linger there. Her skin was so warm it made him think of lazy days on a sailboat, just the two of them, somewhere tropical and remote. He cupped her buttocks, and she pressed herself into him.

His lips followed the line of her neck, teasing her skin with more kisses, his tongue laving a path as he went. She even tasted like sun on a beach, he thought illogically. Hot and captivating. By the time he reached the curve where her shoulder met her neck, he could hardly stand it. Turning her around slowly, he began to kiss the nape of her neck, his fingers finding the top of her dress. The sound of her zipper was soft, but her sigh was even fainter as the back of the garment fell open and he slipped his hands inside.

CHAPTER THIRTEEN

JENNIFER CAUGHT her dress with her hands as it slipped off her shoulders and fell forward. Beck was behind her, kissing her, soft little touches of his mouth against her bare skin. She groaned and closed her eyes, letting the sensation of his touch, his smell, his presence envelope her completely.

She'd never wanted a man as much as she wanted him.

Each time his lips found a new place on her body, a small flame built, her craving for more growing even stronger. He was connecting all the blazes with his tongue and his hands. Sooner or later, the fires would merge and consume her. She knew this as surely as she knew how wrong it was for her to let him continue, but she couldn't stop him…and she couldn't stop herself, either.

She leaned against him as his fingers inched forward then played their way over her bare skin between her bra and panties. The touch was exquisite when he trailed one finger along her rib cage, then nibbled on her neck. A moment later, the flat of his hand encompassed the whole of her abdomen, his palm spreading over her skin with the same searing heat she'd experienced before. When he ran his thumb inside the top of her panties, she actually felt weak.

He murmured against her skin, his mouth lifting for only a second. "You are so incredibly beautiful. And I want you so much."

As his deep voice rumbled, she stared through a half-lidded gaze across his living room. Their reflection in the glass of the patio doors barely registered, but what she saw was enough. The erotic pose—Beck behind, his mouth pressed to her neck, her dress halfway down—made her sway with desire.

Through this fog of heat and touch, she gazed at the window, and slowly, so slowly she hardly noticed at first, something else registered, something so outside the realm of where they were and what they were doing she didn't even make sense of it at first. She closed her eyes against the sight; she wanted nothing to interrupt them. Not reality, not her problems, not his job. She only wanted him, but compelled by an insistence she couldn't ignore, she looked again.

In one corner of the glass his bedroom and a closet door were reflected. Hanging over the top of the door was a lightweight jacket and a pair of pants, both black and neatly pressed. All she could see of the jacket was the back and from that she caught the curving *S* and the slash of a *T*. On the doorknob dangled a bulletproof vest and beside it sat his helmet and boots.

All the components of his SWAT uniform.

She told herself she was acting ridiculous; Beck was kind and loving and considerate—everything her father had never been. She was thinking too much about this. *Close your eyes and kiss him, that's all you have to do. Let him make love to you and forget about it.*

But she couldn't. She couldn't just *make love*. To Jennifer, that action meant commitment and a life with Beck would hold the same pitfalls, even if he wasn't the same man.

She stiffened, and Beck's hands stilled in instant response.

"What's wrong?" he asked.

She swallowed, her throat as tight and constricted as if she were choking. "N-nothing," she fibbed.

He pulled back and slowly turned her around to face him. "I told you once never to lie to a liar. It's pointless." The blue gaze scorched her. "What's wrong, Jennifer?"

With shaking hands she pulled her dress up to cover herself. "I—I don't think I'm ready. That's all."

His eyes widened for a moment with an incredulous expression, but he shuttered it quickly, his voice as neutral as if he were talking someone off a ledge.

"What changed? You were certainly ready a second before."

The answer ran through head. *I saw your uniform and remembered who I'm really with.* But she couldn't tell him that. He'd think she was an even bigger nut than she'd already demonstrated.

She held herself with awkward tension and stared at him. "I changed my mind," she said. "That's my prerogative, isn't it?

His face reflected his hurt, but he nodded once like the gentlemen he was. "Of course it is. I'll get your shawl and take you home. Turn around so I can zip your dress."

She did as he instructed, and when he finished, he lifted his gaze. His puzzled expression cleared as his eyes went to the same thing she'd seen.

He looked back to her. "It's my uniform, isn't it?"

"It's not the uniform itself," she answered. "It's what's behind it. You know that."

"And you're going to let that stand between us?"

"I have to."

"No, you don't *have to.*" His words were chips of ice. "You're making the choice. You and you alone."

THE NEXT FEW DAYS were torture for Beck. A dozen times he picked up the phone to call Jennifer and a dozen times he put it back down. She was the one who'd stopped things. When she was ready, she could call him. Maybe he was being harsh, but she had to make the decision, not him.

Standing on the shoreline in the early-morning sun, Beck crammed his hands into his pockets and stared out over the water. His rod and reel were anchored in the sand at his feet, the line playing out then coming back with the wash of the tide. He wasn't really fishing—the gear was just an excuse to come down to the beach and do something. He'd hoped it might get Jennifer off his mind, but he'd been wrong. It'd take something stronger than a fishing pole and a bucket of bait to get rid of those thoughts.

The line grew taut and Beck watched it for a minute. Deciding there really was something taking the bait, he picked up the rod and gently played it out a bit more, the spool twisting smoothly. Whatever was on the other end swam out farther and took the hook with it, the slack in the line disappearing as the crank handle turned against Beck's palm. With only half his attention, he went through the motions of slowly bringing the fish in, his finger on the line guide, his mind still on Jennifer.

When they'd gone out this past weekend, something had happened between the two of them. Something he couldn't ignore. Up to this point, he'd been attracted, sure, even thought once or twice that he might be falling for her, but now he knew the truth. Nothing was going to dislodge her from the place she'd carved for herself inside his heart. When he'd carried her pale form from the Marina's dining room, he'd been snagged as surely as whatever was on his line. Just remembering the expression in her eyes when she'd asked him to hold her was all it took for him to feel the same wash of need and desire again. The kiss they'd shared later and the anticipation of making love with her had sealed his feelings even more. Jennifer was someone he could love.

Just as quickly, though, he remembered those same brown eyes after she'd spotted his uniform. He'd cursed himself a hundred times for leaving the damn thing out. He'd known how she felt about it—she'd told him, but he just hadn't remembered. It wasn't the uniform itself, of course, it was what it symbolized. She'd wanted to discuss Howard, too. He'd sensed that when they'd talked over drinks, but he'd dodged the issue one more time. Would that always hang over them?

She had a major problem with his job, that much was for sure. But he was falling in love with her and that was just as obvious, at least to him.

What in the hell was he supposed to do?

He reeled the line into the shallow water, then tucked the rod under his arm to snag the floundering amberjack. The yellow scales were bright in the dawn's breaking light. The fish was a small one and with a deft flick of his wrist he freed the barb from its gills, set it back into the water, then watched as it flashed away, free once more.

His thoughts stayed hooked and tangled.

NADINE DIDN'T REALLY like to leave the safety of Seacrest, but at least once a month, Jennifer and Wanda took her on an excursion. Wanda insisted it was good for the older woman to experience different settings, even if she didn't appear to appreciate the outings. It wasn't the best place in the world to bring her mother, but Jennifer had been unable to think of anything better and they ended up at the outlet mall the weekend following her date with Beck. The sprawling complex covered hundreds of elegant shops, and in the center, a group of restaurants served a dozen different cuisines, as well as snacks and drinks.

Jennifer hardly noticed where they were. Her mind had been a sieve the past week, confused thoughts and anxieties passing through her brain with barely enough time for her to think about them before they disappeared. Her nightmares had returned, too, but thank God she hadn't had another panic attack. She'd seen Maria twice, the therapist instructing her on how to handle the problem if it happened again and commiserating with her about the incident in the restaurant.

But what really had Jennifer upset had nothing to do with any of that.

It was Beck. The man was trapped inside her head and nothing she could do would budge him. She'd played their kiss over a thousand times, reenacting the ending with just as many changes. She'd really wanted to make love with him, but she'd stopped it from happening.

And she had the strong suspicion, she'd made an awful mistake. He'd been absolutely right. She needed to move from the past and live her own life.

As they strolled along the covered walkway with Nadine between them, Wanda glanced in Jennifer's direction. "You never said much about your date. How did it go?"

Torn with indecision, Jennifer looked at her friend. She'd wanted to call Wanda all week and cry on her shoulder, but something had held her back. As she caught her friend's caring glance, Jennifer realized what that something was. She knew exactly what Wanda was going to tell her and she was afraid to hear it. She had to talk about it, though. If she didn't, she might explode.

Jennifer took a deep breath and explained it all, including the panic attack. "He was really sweet and kind and after it was all over, he took me back to his place."

Wanda had been frowning as she listened to the details of what had happened, but she smiled when Jennifer mentioned Beck's home. "God, girl, why didn't you start with that little detail instead?"

Jennifer shook her head. "It was a disaster."

"Oh, no! What happened?"

"He kissed me," Jennifer answered. "And I kissed him back. It was…incredible."

"An incredible kiss and it was disaster? I need details to understand that."

"It was too incredible for details," Jennifer answered. "Just trust me on the point, okay?"

"Well, at least tell me what happened next. You can't leave me hanging like this."

Jennifer looked away. A family of tourists were ahead of them, complete with sunglasses, stroller and video camera. They stopped before a jewelry store window, and the mother and father rolled the baby carriage back and forth as they looked into the window. Grandmother stepped back and filmed the event. Jennifer spoke softly. "I stopped it before it went any further."

"Are you crazy?" Wanda's voice rose and the mother of the group ahead glanced back curiously. "Why'd you go and do that?"

"Because I can't have a relationship with him, that's why. All I've been thinking about are—" She stopped abruptly, her eyes going to her mother's face. Nadine was staring into the distance, totally unaware of her surroundings.

"Yes?" Wanda asked gently.

Jennifer forced herself to relax. "—are the reasons I don't need to get involved with him." She held up her hand and folded her fingers down one at a time. "His life is bizarre. I don't trust him. He's unpredictable and he keeps secrets.'' She stopped and dropped her hand. ''Want more?''

Wanda didn't answer. She held up her own hand in response and mimicked Jennifer's movements. ''He's as handsome as the devil. He's smart and kind and has a well-paying, steady job. He's nuts about you. Do *I* need to go on? That's more reasons than you had. I win.'' She shook her head and stared at Jennifer with a disbelieving expression. ''What's wrong with you? Most of us spend our lives lookin' for a man like him and you're standing here thinkin' up reasons not to like him. I don't believe it.''

They passed an expensive leather shop then a candy store before Jennifer could answer. ''I can't do it,'' she answered. ''I just can't do it.''

Wanda stopped their progress by putting her hand on Jennifer's arm. Nadine moved ahead of them to stare into a window display of beach towels and swimsuits. ''What are you so damned afraid of?'' Her black eyes bored into Jennifer's. ''The man is good and he'd be good *for* you. It's past time you start to live, Jennifer. Why don't you want to do that?''

''I do,'' she said immediately. ''But he's not the one to do it with.''

Wanda put her hands on her hips and shook her head. ''Ever since you met him, you've said that, but I don't understand why. So what if he's a cop? So what if his life might interfere with your ordered little plans? What's more important? Living or planning to live?'' Her forehead wrinkled and she pointed at Nadine, three steps ahead of them. ''Look at your mama up there. That could be you or me tomorrow. We could get hit by a truck and it'd all be over. We could be dead or worse—be like her. Your life is yours to live, *right now*. Don't spend your life waiting for the perfect man or the perfect time. That's never going to happen, because perfect doesn't exist.'' She dropped her hand and shook her head, her eyes almost sorrowful as they met Jennifer's. ''You're insane if you let this guy get away.''

They spent the rest of the afternoon meandering through the shops, but Jennifer couldn't remember which ones they'd gone in when she got home that night. Wanda's words refused to leave her alone.

And Beck's presence haunted her dreams.

BECK WAS STARING out the window at the baking asphalt in the parking lot when Lena came into the squad room on Thursday evening and sat down beside his desk. He'd been back at work for two whole weeks, but his heart wasn't in it. Lena looked as if she had the same problem. She had dark circles under her eyes and a worried air about her.

He leaned back in his chair, the springs creaking. ''Are you okay? You look like *you* need a vacation.''

She smiled briefly at his attempt at humor, then shook her head. ''I'm tired,'' she said. ''I had a seminar in Pensacola last night and I didn't get home until after midnight. I was supposed to pick up Nate at the airport and didn't make it. He wasn't happy.''

"What are you doing here then? Go find him and make up.''

"It's not that easy, Beck. You don't understand....''

Beck made a sympathetic sound in the back of his throat, but he wasn't really paying attention. He was thinking of Jennifer. Only when Lena spoke sharply did he realize she'd been talking about something for quite some time.

He grinned at her sheepishly. "I'm sorry, Lena, but I wasn't listening. What did you say?''

She looked at him strangely. "My God, you are on another planet. I just gave you news that ought to have you jumping up and down and instead you didn't even hear me.''

"Well, tell me again.''

"I just put Randy on probation.''

He stared at her in amazement. "Are you shi—''

She interrupted him. "This is a heads up, Beck. He's not happy and he's looking for someone to blame. If I were you, I'd lay low for a while and watch my back.''

"I appreciate the warning, but I'm more interested in hearing why. What finally brought you to this point?''

She looked at him steadily. "I think you know the answer to that question.''

He returned her look then nodded slowly. Last week the team had had a party at the home of Bradley Thompson. The cookout around the sergeant's home had been relaxed and pleasant until Randy had shown up. Drunk and obnoxious when he'd arrived, things had only gotten worse as the party had progressed. Linc had finally driven the young sniper home to sleep it off.

"I talked to him on Monday about what happened at Bradley's. He apologized and said he didn't know what got into him." Her face took on an expression of regret. "I told him that wasn't good enough. We have to be ready to roll twenty-four hours a day. Blowing off some steam is one thing, but passed out drunk is something else. He couldn't have worked if we'd gotten a call. It would have taken more than a day to get that much alcohol out of his bloodstream. His hands would have been worthless. I put him on probation. If he screws up again, he's out. I just thought you might want to know." She stood up slowly, then looked down at Beck. "He said it wasn't really his fault and that you were behind my decision. He's loaded for bear, Beck. Be careful out there, okay?"

Beck nodded once, then the phone rang and Lena left the office. With one hand, he picked up the report he'd been reading and with the other he reached for the phone. "Winters," he said into the receiver, his attention on the papers he held.

"Beck? This is Jennifer."

"Jennifer!" A rush of feeling hit him at the sound of her voice. He'd given up hope that she would call, and now here she was, sounding as if she'd made up her mind about something important and wasn't going to be deterred. "How are you?"

"I'm fine," she said. "Just fine. How's it been going since we had dinner?"

The small talk was curious considering her tone, but he went with it. "Not that easy. I was getting into sleeping late. I could've handled that some more." *Especially if you'd been beside me,* he thought unexpectedly.

"That's good...." She stopped, her words drifting into silence. He waited patiently and finally she spoke again. "Listen, Beck, I'm calling to say...well, to say I'm sorry. About the other night, the last time we were together."

"There's nothing to be sorry for."

"Then why do I feel so awful?"

"I don't know why, but I'd be willing to take a guess."

"And that would be..."

Gathering his thoughts, he hesitated for a bit. "Maybe because you didn't really want to stop. Maybe you wished you'd let things go on to their natural conclusion."

"Is that how *you* feel?"

''You know that's how I feel,'' he said. ''You didn't have to call to find that out.''

She paused, and the soft, even measure of her breathing came over the phone. ''You could be right. Whatever the reason, I've been doing a lot of thinking about it, and I—I'd like to show you how I really feel about things. I'd like another chance if you're interested.''

The image of her silky tanned legs, her shining hair, her full, sensual lips came to him instantly, but an even stronger impression—a realization, actually—overlaid those physical attributes, as wonderful as they were. No matter what happened between them in the future, she had become a part of him he didn't want to lose. It was a scary thought, but there was nothing he could do about it.

His answer was simple. ''I'm interested.''

''Could I cook dinner for you Saturday night?''

''I can't think of anything I'd like better.''

She laughed at his heartfelt expression, a self-conscious note in the sound that made her even more appealing. ''Just one other thing,'' she said. ''I'd like to cook it at your place. Do you mind?''

It seemed an odd request, but he didn't care. ''Of course, I don't mind. But I'll warn you now. I'm pretty low in the pots and pans department.''

''It doesn't matter,'' she answered. ''I'll put everything together at my place and just heat it up over there. I...well, it's kind of hard to explain, but I wanted to come over there.''

As she spoke again, further comprehension came over him. She had something she wanted to prove to herself, and maybe to him, too, although that wasn't necessary. ''I understand,'' he answered. ''And it's not a problem, so don't worry about it.''

''See you at seven?''

''See you at seven.''

Beck hung up the phone, leaned back in his chair and stared out the squad room window. In the hot morning light, the palm trees seemed to shimmer. He stared at them but thought of Jennifer. What had changed her mind?

Whatever it was, for the moment, it didn't matter. Glancing down at his desk, he saw the stopwatch he used for calls. Impulsively, he picked it up and set it for 7:00 p.m. on Saturday, the green digital numbers changing the minute he touched the button, their countdown beginning. He felt each tick echo in his pulse. Forty-eight hours and counting.

CHAPTER FOURTEEN

JENNIFER HAD MADE her special shrimp dish a thousand times. It was her favorite company entree, but this time something had definitely gone wrong. She stared in dismay at the lumpy cheese sauce, then with a groan, she lifted the pot and dumped it—sauce and all—in the sink. She'd just have to start over. Again.

Reassembling the ingredients, she shook her head over her cooking disaster and stared at her recipe. She knew exactly where the problem lay—it was with the cook. She was rattled and distracted. Making the decision to call Beck had been a big one for her, and she still wasn't sure she was doing the right thing. Talking to Wanda had helped, then she'd discussed the topic with Maria during one of their sessions, too. Strangely enough, it was her mother who'd given her the courage to finally telephone him.

Her eyes focused, her mind almost there, Nadine had listened carefully the previous Wednesday as Jennifer talked about Beck.

"It sounds as if you like him," her mother said timidly. "Is he really a nice boy, Jennifer?"

She'd smiled over the *boy* part. Beck was a man—

that was more than clear. "He's wonderful," she answered. "And he's been very supportive. I think you'd like him, too."

"I'm sure I would if you do." Nadine smiled so sweetly it stole Jennifer's breath. "Falling in love with someone is very important, you know. You have to be careful about who holds your heart."

Jennifer left the nursing home with those words ringing in her mind. The next day, she'd picked up the phone and called Beck. Now here she was, burning her cheese sauce and getting nervous.

Concentrating harder, she grabbed the chunk of Asiago and began to grate again.

WHEN HE OPENED the door, Beck wasn't prepared. He'd expected Jennifer to be on the other side—the stopwatch had beeped a few minutes before—but actually seeing her at his door, waiting just for him, was almost unnerving. He'd faced guns and irate husbands, hostage situations and suicide takers but none of them had made him as nervous as he was right now. Maybe he'd thought she would back out or maybe he'd decided he'd dreamed her phone call. Whatever it was, as she stood there and smiled at him, his heartbeat suddenly accelerated, kicking inside his chest as if a .45 were pointed at him.

In an effort to distract himself, he looked at the dress she wore. It was simple, a white sleeveless thing. Her legs were bare, and their tanned perfection didn't help his jitters at all. It worked the opposite way, in fact, so he fastened on the details. She had on sandals, but she'd changed her polish. This time her toenails were red and so was her lipstick. He found himself wondering if that signified something important.

He hoped it did.

She spoke warily, her smile tentative. "May I come in? Or is something wrong?"

"God, yes. I'm sorry...." Feeling like a fool, he opened the door wider and stepped aside, waving his arm toward the entry. "Please, come in. Whatever you're carrying smells outstanding."

"I hope it tastes that way, too." She eased past him and headed toward the small walk-through kitchen, talking over her shoulder. "It'll be a miracle if it's worth eating. I'm going to chill it while I finish making the salads."

Closing the door, Beck hurried to catch up with her. By the time she'd set the dish inside his almost empty refrigerator, he was standing right behind her. "I'm sure it'll be terrific. Anything short of a Hot Pocket is gourmet to me."

She turned to reply and bumped into him with a tiny, "Oh."

He hadn't meant to be so close—or had he? As Beck raised his hands to steady her, he wasn't sure. Either way, when he touched her, his fingers sliding against the bare satin of her arm, something happened between them.

If someone had asked him later to describe that moment, Beck would not have been able to do it. He didn't have the words in his vocabulary. All he knew was that he had to kiss Jennifer. It sounded unbelievable—and it felt that way, too—but he recognized the power of the urge for what it was. Nothing could have kept him from her. Nothing. Lowering his head to hers, he put his mouth against her lips and everything else fell into place. His hands on her hips, her fingers against his chest, their bodies one against the other.

Dropping the lettuce to the counter, she stiffened in surprise. But almost immediately she moved closer to him, her arms going up to link around his neck, her firm curves molding to his hips and thighs with an obvious response. She was perfect and he marveled at the way they fit together. From the very first moment he'd seen her, Beck had felt a connection with Jennifer and now, as she kissed him so freely, he experienced the strength of that invisible attachment. He didn't understand it and had no idea where it came from, but it was as real as the room in which they stood. He'd heard of two people being made for each other and scoffed.

He would never do that again.

They held the embrace for a few more minutes, then Beck pulled back and looked down at her. He wanted to lift her up, carry her to his bedroom and make love to her. He didn't want dinner, he didn't want dessert. He didn't want to open the chilled bottle of Chablis she'd asked him to buy. All he wanted was her, but he couldn't say that. Jennifer was different from the other women he'd dated. She was too smart and too beautiful and too elegant to drag into the bedroom without making sure everything was as flawless as she was. He'd almost done that before and it'd been a disaster. He wanted to do it right this time. She deserved the very best he could give her and rushing to bed wouldn't be it.

She met his gaze with her dark-brown eyes, then she brought her hands forward and placed them on either side of his face. Her touch was light and delicate and he could hardly bear to feel it because it made him ache for more. With her fingertips barely brushing his skin, a silent spark of anticipation flared between them. It was swift and electrical.

"Let's skip dinner," she said in a husky voice. "Suddenly something else sounds like a lot more fun."

SHE'D NEVER BEEN so direct with a man in her life; it was totally out of character for Jennifer. But feeling the blue heat of Beck's gaze and reading the desire behind the attraction they both obviously felt, nothing else made sense. She wanted him as much as he wanted her, and she'd done enough thinking about it.

She wanted action. Whether it was the right thing or not, she didn't care. She'd already decided.

He smiled slowly, an expression that went straight into her heart and warmed her even more—something she'd have thought impossible at this point.

"I agree completely," he said. "But I have to ask—you're sure?"

"I'm here, aren't I?"

"Yes, but—"

She moved her fingers to his lips and silenced him gently. "Don't ask me anymore," she instructed softly. "Just kiss me, okay?"

He did as she requested, and once again, his lips covered hers. The moment seemed to last an eternity but maybe she just wanted it to feel that way. Without taking his mouth away, he bent down and swept her into his arms. In a dozen long strides they were in his bedroom. He set her down beside the bed, his hands going to the back of her dress. With his eyes never leaving hers, he slowly eased the zipper down. The air-conditioning in the apartment suddenly kicked on and cold air from the vent overhead skimmed over her bare skin. Jennifer shivered once, the juxtaposition of the chill to Beck's heated touch almost more than she could handle.

He left her dress hanging on her shoulders, then lifted his hands to his shirt and started to unbutton it. She wanted to do it herself, but Jennifer couldn't move. She watched as the shirt fell open to reveal his tanned and muscular chest. She'd never been with someone so imposing, so overpowering. If her knees hadn't been against the bed, she might have backed up to increase the distance between them. Beck seemed to take all the space in the room and compress it into something flammable. Only when he shrugged out of his shirt did her paralysis end. Her hands went to his bare skin and she spread her palms over his chest. She almost snatched her hands away, his body was so hot, but she left them there, unable to pull herself away. Under her touch, she was amazed to feel his heart thumping almost as fast as her own.

She lifted her eyes to his and his blue gaze, so cold in the past, was burning. "Turn around," he said hoarsely. "Let me take off your dress."

Once again, she did exactly as he said, and when the ivory sheath fell to the floor, she pivoted in the circle of his arms to face him.

Gently reaching out, he traced the swell of her right breast, taking a slow, torturous route before he slipped his finger into the valley of her cleavage. Her pulse leapt. How could he touch her so simply and make her feel as if she were about to explode? He brought his hand up and let the finger lightly flicker over her other side, then he reached out with both hands and cupped the weight of her breasts, his thumbs scorching her nipples through the lace of her bra. She caught her breath in her throat and froze.

She felt dizzy and disoriented and completely undone. As they sunk toward the bed, their arms wrapped around each other, she put her hands against his back and encountered the strength of his muscles. Only then—when her touch registered—did she finally understand what was going on.

Beck made her feel safe. He was so tall and so strong, she felt protected from any danger. No one had ever done this for her before and she opened herself up to him with a sigh of release.

He sensed her acquiescence. Shedding the rest of his clothes and removing what was left of hers, his hands danced over her bare skin with a faster, more urgent need. She responded in kind, her fingers exploring the ridges and cords of his arms and legs and back. Each place she touched felt the same; rock solid and hard.

Only his mouth was soft and tender. Everywhere he could, he was kissing her, his lips drawing a crazy quilt pattern of desire that grew with every second. His hands quickly followed and with each feathered caress, he brought her closer and closer to the brink of a climax. No longer able to control herself, she pressed against him and urged him into a faster pace. But she didn't need to tell him; he read her body as easily as he did everything else. He reached into the bedside table, then she heard the foil tear as he took out a condom. A moment later, he slipped inside her with gentle care and built the rhythm into the kind of frenzied tempo they both needed. With the part of her brain that wasn't on fire, Jennifer noted this in amazement. How did he know how to please her so well? How could he tell what to do and when to do it?

She only wondered for a moment. His powerful thrusts sent her mind spinning into an abyss of pleasure. For what seemed like a very long time, she stayed there, untethered by anything but the thrill of the building heat between them. It was more incredible than she'd even imagined. She couldn't have envisaged the feeling because nothing in her past had come even close. The explosion of her climax was just as astounding. Totally unprepared, she let the sensual wave carry her off.

When she drifted back down, she had a single thought. It came from a place deep within her, but Jennifer knew—as all women do—that the impression was as real as the bed she was lying in.

Nothing in her life would ever be the same again.

SHE WOKE UP in the middle of the night. For one short second, Jennifer didn't know where she was and she panicked, a dark sweep of anxiety and fear washing over her in a haze of black and red. Before the fear could overwhelm her, she brought herself to calmness—just as Maria had taught her—and the jittery confusion fled. Her breathing slowed and her heartbeat did as well. She felt proud of herself. The bad dreams had almost stopped, and she hadn't had a real panic attack since the night she'd been with Beck at the restaurant. Maria had really helped.

But the man beside her had helped even more. Jennifer turned her head and looked at Beck's chiseled profile in the darkness.

He was extraordinary. That's the only word she could think of to describe him. Patient and kind, he'd insisted she see Maria, then he'd gone on to help her even more. Now they were lovers, and in her heart, Jennifer acknowledged she wanted to go beyond that. She could see him as the father of the children she'd always longed for, as the man who mowed the yard inside the picket fence. Refusing to allow any negative thoughts to destroy the growing image, she let herself play with it for a little while longer. He'd go with her to visit Nadine, he'd attend all the school parties with her, they'd go shopping and to the movies and out to eat. They'd be a couple. They'd be a family.

Easing slowly from beneath his arm, Jennifer rose from the bed and grabbed the shirt Beck had been wearing. She slipped into it and stared down at him, telling herself she was nuts for letting the fantasy build. She couldn't stop, though. As his chest rose and fell, she stared at him with longing. Was there any way this relationship could work? Or was she being ridiculous?

She padded through the darkness of his apartment and into the kitchen. She'd left on the light above the cooktop. The dim illumination served to build the shadows more than anything else, but with it as her guide, she opened the refrigerator and saw the casserole, still tempting even though it was cold. Suddenly she was ravenous. She reached into the oval dish and plucked out a shrimp. Just as she stuck it into her mouth, a noise sounded behind her. Her hand at her lips, she turned.

"Am I going to have to arrest you for burglary?" Beck stood at the doorway to the kitchen, his huge form filling the entry as he spoke. "I believe that dish was made for two—and here you are snitching the shrimp out of it."

She grinned and swallowed, putting on a mock expression of guilt. "I guess you caught me." Reaching over, she snagged another shrimp and held it out to him. "If I share, would you go easy on me?"

He took one step into the kitchen then took the shrimp from her fingers and tossed it into his mouth. "My God, that's wonderful," he said as he chewed. "Can we have it for breakfast?"

"Why not eat it right now?" she countered playfully. "We could call it a midnight snack."

He acted as if he were considering her offer, then slowly he shook his head. "I don't think so. I've got something better in mind."

Before she could answer, he took another step and whisked her into his arms. They didn't even make it to the bedroom this time.

BECK DIDN'T WANT to release Jennifer. Not for a minute, not forever… Despite his protests, though, she slid from his arms a little later and disappeared into the bathroom, closing the door behind her, the sound of running water coming on right after. He immediately felt cold and alone. His reaction should have surprised him—but it didn't. There was no other way he could feel considering the past few hours. If he'd thought she'd gotten under his skin before, he'd had no idea what he was really in for. Jennifer shared his passion, and each touch, each kiss, each look had sealed his feelings for her even more. There had to be a way he could convince her they should be together—forever. He didn't know what it would be, but Beck stared at the line of light seeping under the bathroom door and vowed to find a way. Now that they'd reached this point, he wouldn't let her go. He *couldn't* let her go. He wanted to think she might agree.

A loud pounding on his front door jerked Beck from his reverie. Glancing toward the clock with a frown, he read the time. It was two in the morning! What in the hell? He grabbed his pants, thrust his legs into them and headed for the door, a thousand possibilities going through his mind, none of them making any sense. Sometimes when they caught a call, Bradley Thompson would swing by and pick him up, but Beck got a phone call first or at the least a page. Whoever was beating on the door was impatient and angry, too—adjectives that definitely didn't fit the able assistant commander.

"Hang on, hang on. I'm coming!" Beck crossed the living room to the small hallway closet and unlocked it swiftly, removing his service revolver from the top shelf where he kept it. He checked the weapon once then crammed it into the back waistband of his slacks. He didn't know who was on the other side, but with Jennifer around, he wasn't about to take any chances. Two strides later, he threw open the front door then stared in shock, a sweep of anger hitting him like a wave from the Gulf.

JENNIFER TURNED OFF the bathroom light, opened the door and headed back into the bedroom. She was at the edge of the bed when she realized it was empty, and grinned. Beck must have returned to the shrimp. Calling out his name, she started into the living room, then stopped abruptly, the sound of loud voices in the entry halting her footsteps and filling her with concern. Whoever was talking was more than just upset, she realized belatedly. He was furious and from the tone of his voice prepared to do something about it.

"This is all your fault, Winters! You've screwed me, and I'm not going to put up with it. Your bullshit has gotten me in enough trouble!"

The rage in the other man's voice was deep and penetrating, and Jennifer felt it all the to her toes. She hadn't heard that kind of undisguised fury since she'd left her father's home.

"Randy, this isn't the time or the place. If you have a problem with me, let's work it out at the station. I'd be happy to talk to you about it then—"

"I'm sure you would!" The voice was slurred, but the emotion wasn't. It was all too clear and Jennifer shivered. "You got Lena on your side up there and all the rest of your asshole buddies! They'd stick up for you and look down their noses at me, like they always do. Uh-uh, Winters. It's you and me, right here, right now."

Jennifer froze against the wall. The man was obviously one of the SWAT team members. She thought of what Beck had called him. *Randy*... Then she remembered. Randy Tamirisa. He was the sniper. She'd read his name in the newspapers and had heard Beck speak of him before.

Randy Tamirisa was the man who'd shot Howard.

Beck spoke again. His tone was neutral and unengaged, but now that she knew him better, she could hear, beneath the professional attitude, something deeper he was trying hard to hold back.

"Don't do something you're gonna regret, Randy. You're drunk and out of line. You don't know what you're doing."

"I know exactly what I'm doing, you son of a bitch. Just like I knew what I was doing when I took that shot at the school."

Something told her she didn't want to hear what was coming next, but Jennifer was trapped. In more ways than one.

"You *didn't* know what you were doing then and you don't know now." Some of the emotion Beck had been concealing seeped out, his voice going deep and husky. "Don't blame me because you're feeling guilty now! You took that shot without Lena's approval and you shouldn't have."

Jennifer gasped softly, then held her breath in her lungs, her pulse suddenly pounding as shock and disbelief washed over her in a dizzying wave. God, why hadn't Beck told her about this? Before she could think about it more, the sniper spoke again.

"I did my job. That idiot was gonna shoot someone."

"You didn't know that for sure." Beck was now openly angry. "You're trigger-happy, Tamirisa, and that's the only truth we need to talk about here. You have no business on the team."

"Get real, Winters. You're jealous. I was man enough to take the shot, and that's something you'll never be. You're a desk jockey, you're not even a real SWAT man. You're telling Lena shit about me just to screw me over."

Jennifer heard the sound of shuffling and a dull thud, the noise a body makes as it hits an immovable object. It didn't take much imagination to realize what had happened. Beck had obviously grabbed the other man and pushed him. The wall she was leaning against vibrated in response.

Beck's voice was tight, barely in control, as he spoke again. "I'm not the first man through the door anymore, but I'll tell you one thing—you made the mistake that day, buddy. You and you alone. That perp didn't need to die. It could have been resolved."

Jennifer closed her eyes and swayed, the whole ugly scene turning her inside out. Howard's face swam in her vision. Something had told her there was more to the story, but Beck had convinced her otherwise. He'd made it sound like the team had done the right thing when all along he'd thought otherwise. Why in heaven's name hadn't he just told her the truth? The obvious answer came swiftly: he couldn't have. It didn't work that way and she was incredibly blind not to have realized that fact before now. His job would *never* permit the whole truth between them.

The man spoke again, his words coming out strangled. "I didn't kill that bastard, Winters. You did! If you'd done *your* job right, he'd have come out and no one woulda gotten shot."

Another thud rattled the wall, a groan of pain echoing right behind it. A dragging sound came next, then the noise of the front door opening. A thump, another moan, then Beck's voice, more angry and intense than Jennifer had ever heard it.

"Go home and sober up and take your goddamn lies with you."

The slamming door shook the entire apartment, but that wasn't the reason Jennifer was trembling.

Moments later, Beck was walking toward her. But he took one look at her face and stopped short. She knew why, too. She was shocked and horrified and sick to her stomach, each and every emotion written in her expression. They'd just made love and in her mind if nowhere else, she'd committed herself to him. Now she knew the facts, and they were just what she'd been afraid of. Nothing in Beck's world made any sense. She and the people she worked with held meetings, had lunches, argued and complained. Beck's co-workers showed up in the middle of the night, stressed out and drunk, to fight over someone else's death!

How long would it be before the inevitable happened? When would Beck be the one out of control? It would happen sooner or later, she knew, and then once again, her life would be where it had started. Her escape all those years ago meaningless.

With bile rising in her throat, Jennifer realized the truth that had come crashing through that door along with Randy Tamirisa. There could be no future between her and Beck. The chaos and confusion of his existence was something she'd never be able to handle. She'd known this at first, but she'd put it aside because she'd fallen in love with him.

Beck's life was insane, and if Jennifer had ever thought she could be with him...then she was crazy, too.

CHAPTER FIFTEEN

CURSING SOUNDLY, Beck held out his hand and came closer to Jennifer. Her eyes were enormous and filled with a betrayal that cut straight into his heart. "Jennifer, sweetheart..."

"Stop right there." Her voice held no room for argument, and he did as she instructed. "Don't come another step. I mean it."

Automatically, he went into his negotiating mode. He nodded slowly, his expression neutral. "Of course. I'll stop. Just let me explain—"

"No!" Her one-word answer was violent and vehement. "There's nothing to explain. I heard all I needed to hear."

"But it wasn't the truth—"

"You don't even know what that is." She shuffled backward from him, her fingers locked on the shirt she wore, her knuckles as white as her face. "You said you did everything you could when Howard was killed."

"And that's still the case."

"But not the full story..."

"I didn't want him to die—"

She shook her head. "You know what? I believe you! You're a good man and I know you well enough now to know you didn't want that—"

"Then why—"

Her eyes flared wide. "Because I can't live with this craziness. I wanted to know what happened that day and I begged you to tell me. But even when we got to know each other better, you didn't come clean! It's not that, though. It's—"

He didn't let her finish. In a flash, he closed the distance between them. Her back against the bedroom door, Jennifer had nowhere to go, and all she could do was look up at him helplessly as he trapped her, his hands on the wall at either side of her head.

"What did you expect, Jennifer? Did you want to hear every little detail? Even if I'd wanted to give them to you, what's the point? Dammit it to hell, I see death and violence everywhere I go. Is that really what you want to hear about when we're together?"

"It's more than that!" she cried. "My father ruined our lives with his secrets and lies and upheaval. It was constant. We never knew what was going on, with him or in our own lives, and I said I'd never live that way again."

"Well, here's a news flash, Jennifer. Life isn't always tied up in neat little bundles that you can stick in numbered boxes. Howard French was killed because our sniper thought he was going to shoot Juan Canales. I disagreed. I thought Tamirisa should have waited. But I could have been wrong. And if I had been, and Juan had died, what would you have thought of me then?''

Angrily he shook his head and didn't wait for her to answer. ''Don't you understand, Jennifer? Life is always going to be full of questions and unanswered problems. Nothing is certain, hell, our *existence* isn't even certain.''

''But you could have told me you didn't agree with the sniper. We could have at least talked about it. That would have helped me.''

''I am a member of the team.'' He spoke each word distinctly as he dropped his arms and stepped back. ''And I owe that team all the loyalty I can muster. Our lives depend on each other, and if we screw up, it's our problem to deal with. Ours and no one else's. I didn't explain what happened because you wouldn't have understood, just like you don't understand now. You see everything through the filter of your past even when it doesn't apply.''

Her face shuttered, the expression going cold and distant. ''What are you saying?''

''I'm saying I'm not your father—''

''I know that—''

''Then realize what it means! I'm a different man but because of our jobs, there are going to be similarities. He kept secrets because he had to and so do I. But there's a damn good reason for that, and if you gave it some thought, you might begin to figure out why.''

She blinked slowly, then turned her head and stared into the darkness of his living room. Her throat moved as she swallowed, then she faced him once again. Her eyes glimmered with unshed tears. The hurt and distrust behind her gaze cut so deeply, he felt a physical pain. He wanted to start over, to try to explain better, but she stopped him.

''I understand all I need to. Living that way ruined my mother's life and ended my brother's. I won't let it do the same to me.''

Once more, Beck began to reply, but the worst thing that *could* happen, did happen. The beeper on his waistband went off. He glanced down and cursed. Another priority call. When he lifted his head, Jennifer simply looked at him.

''I have to leave—''

''You always have to leave.'' Her voice was almost sad, and Beck heard the goodbye in the words, even though she didn't say it. His chest went tight.

''Stay here,'' he pleaded. ''We can talk about this some more when I get back.''

She shook her head, her dark hair brushing her shoulders with a weary whisper. ''I won't be here when you come home. There's nothing else to say.''

SHE DRESSED in silence behind the bathroom door and when she came out, Beck had left, as she'd expected.

There was a hastily scribbled note on the floor of the living room that began ''Dear Jennifer...'' but she didn't bother to read it. It wouldn't matter anyway. Nothing he could say would change the situation. His life couldn't be hers. Ever. Numbly, she left the apartment and went to her car, getting inside and driving off without a clue as to where she was headed. Only when she pulled up in front of Seacrest did she understand where she'd driven.

Climbing out of the car, she made her way through the empty parking lot and up to the double glass doors. Like most of its occupants, the building seemed to be sleeping. The lights were muted, the halls were empty and even the ever present music was turned down so low it was almost silent. Jennifer walked past the abandoned reception desk and started down the hallway to her mother's room. When she passed the nurses' station, she saw the aide who manned the desk. The woman had her back to Jennifer and was pouring herself a cup of coffee. Jennifer went by without saying a word then she entered her mother's room still not knowing why she was there.

The revelation came to her without any warning. Seacrest was where she came when she got upset. It wasn't the hardship she'd always thought it was. It was the exact opposite. Being with her mother brought Jennifer peace when the outside world overwhelmed her. The realization astonished her, but Jennifer couldn't deny it. Visiting Nadine wasn't a burden—it was a gift—for both of them.

Nadine was asleep, but as Jennifer approached the bed, her mother's eyes opened. She smiled gently. "Jennifer, come in, sweetheart...."

Jennifer's heartbeat fluttered as Nadine spoke her name. She knew her. The awareness in her mother's eyes felt so good to Jennifer, she almost hated to acknowledge it. Who knew when it would happen again? Or even *if* it would. Inevitably there would be a time when that was no longer a possibility at all. She walked closer to the bed and dropped a kiss on Nadine's forehead. Beneath Jennifer's lips, her mother's skin felt as thin and fragile as the single wing of a moth.

"Hi, Mom. I didn't mean to wake you up. I'm sorry."

"It's okay." Nadine smiled again. "I was having a dream about your father."

Jennifer wearily shook her head and sat down on the chair beside the bed. "A nightmare, you mean?"

"Oh no, it was a wonderful dream. We were both young and so much in love it hurt. Kinda like you and your young man are."

Startled by her mother's words, Jennifer looked at her sharply. She wasn't sure what surprised her the most. Her mother's lucidity, her reference to Beck, or the explanation of the dream. She picked one at random. "You think we're in love?"

"You told me you were the other day. That hasn't changed, has it?"

"I—I don't know."

Her mother sat up, her hair shining in the light drifting in from the hallway. "You look upset. Did you have a fight?"

Miserably, Jennifer nodded.

"Tell me about it, darling."

"I'm not sure I can. It's complicated."

Nadine nodded slowly. "Love usually is. It certainly was that way between your father and me."

Jennifer held her breath. Her mother was making so much sense, it scared her. She'd had clear moments in the past, but they hadn't had a conversation like this in more than a month and even then, Nadine hadn't been this coherent. Jennifer asked the question and prayed there would be an answer that made sense. "What do you mean, Mom?"

She shook her head, the strands of silver whispering against the bed linens. "He wasn't a nice man," she said. "But I loved him so much it hurt. I think I hated our life because he wouldn't give me all of it."

Disappointment came over Jennifer. Nadine *wasn't* thinking straight.

Her mother turned to look at her more closely. "You don't understand what I'm saying, do you?"

"No, Mom. I don't think I do."

She seemed to struggle to find the right words, her forehead wrinkling. "I was always despondent whenever he had to leave. And when he came home, I wanted to know all the details, but he wouldn't tell me. I pushed him so much he got bitter and resentful, then angry. That's the man you knew. When he was younger he wasn't that way. He had changed by the time you were born.'' She picked at the sheet. ''I think that's why Danny was so confused. His father had been one man, then slowly he became someone else. That's not something a child can understand. But I didn't, either. Not until later. I didn't know he was trying to protect me....'' Her eyes fluttered down.

As she'd spoken, Jennifer had pulled the chair closer. She spoke urgently. ''Mom? Tell me more, please...Mom?''

''I'm sleepy,'' Nadine answered in a fretful voice. Opening her eyes once more, she looked at Jennifer suspiciously. ''What kind of nurse are you to come in here and wake me up? Leave me alone, young lady.''

Jennifer's shoulders slumped in dismay. Nadine had been there—really been there—for what? Twenty seconds, maybe less? Jennifer's frustration bloomed. She had questions to ask, things she needed to know. What had Nadine meant about Jennifer's father trying to protect her? Protect her from what? Jennifer wanted to reach over and shake her sleeping mother, but that was pointless, and she knew it. Without any warning, the futility and disappointment of the night suddenly swept over her. Like an avalanche off a mountain, blinding and unstoppable, all her emotions exploded at once, and there was nothing Jennifer could do but hurt. She laid her head on her mother's bed and began to weep.

BY THE TIME she got home, Jennifer was drained. It was almost 5:00 a.m., and she could hardly see she was so exhausted. Staying up all night was for college students. A mature, responsible woman had no business crawling into her apartment in the same clothes she'd put on the day before. This wasn't how it was supposed to be, she thought wearily, unlocking the door and stepping inside. Was the fantasy just that? Would she never have the stable life, the children, the home, the husband she wanted?

She felt bruised and battered, her body aching as much as her mind. Her tears threatened to begin again, but she held them in. By the time she threw back the covers and climbed into bed, she was shivering with fatigue. The feeling was as much mental as it was physical, but when she closed her eyes, sleep refused to come, just as she'd known it would. She almost welcomed the insomnia, though; who knew what kind of nightmares she'd have.

Surrendering to the inevitable, she plumped the pillows behind her back and reached for the remote control. The bluish light of the television bathed the room and bed with faint illumination, the voice of the Channel Seven reporter coming along with the picture. Jennifer always watched the show when she was getting dressed. She shook her head, then found herself focusing on the set, the newswoman's expression and excited hand gestures more agitated than usual. In the background, a modest, low-rise commercial building filled the screen. Jennifer recognized it immediately. The office housed the salon where she got her hair cut. The reporter spoke with staccato rapidity.

"I'm standing in front of the Renaissance Center in downtown Destin. Earlier this morning, police were dispatched to this location following an automatic alarm call. Shortly after they arrived, shots were fired at the officers.

"The Emerald Coast SWAT team is on-site. This structure contains a beauty salon, a drugstore and a demolition firm. The armed man inside is threatening to blow up the building, using material he located in the demolition company's offices."

Jennifer's mouth dropped open with horrified disbelief. This was the call Beck had gotten—it had to be! She threw off the blanket and crawled to the foot of the bed closer to where the television set rested on the dresser. The voice of the Channel Seven anchor broke in.

"Ginger, do you know if there's anyone else in the building right now?"

The reporter put a hand to her ear. "We're just not sure, Jamie. There could be people trapped inside, but the only persons we've actually witnessed running to the back door area were SWAT members protecting one man who went inside. We believe him to be the negotiator. We're assuming he's talking to the alleged gunman and trying to get him out of there. The media representative for the team, Sarah Greenberg, has refused to comment on the situation."

"Oh, my God…" Jennifer whispered the words, but the room seemed to hold them and magnify their sound, along with her fear. "Oh, God…oh, God…" Her prayer dissolved into silence, her tight throat making it impossible to say more.

"Exactly what kind of material is in the construction office?"

The reporter nodded her head as she heard the anchor's question, her expression avid with anticipation of a bigger story. "We don't know exactly, Jamie. We contacted the owner of the firm, Anderson Destruction, and he confirmed a job had been canceled at the last minute on Friday. Because of that, he took some type of explosive material to the office for, as he put it, 'safe keeping.' Regardless of how this ends, charges may be filed against the firm."

"So it's possible this situation could turn deadly?"

The woman nodded vigorously. "Absolutely, Jamie. In fact, they've cleared and barricaded a square block around where we're standing now. We'll stay in touch and keep our viewers as informed as we can."

Now only inches from the television set, Jennifer

reached out toward the screen, her fingers touching the front of the building behind the reporter. "Oh, please…" she breathed. "Keep him safe, please… keep him safe…"

"We'll get back to you, Ginger."

The woman nodded once and turned, then all at once, behind her, a loud explosion rippled through one side of the office. The windows at that end disintegrated, instantly sending glass and debris flying through the air. A corner of the roof lifted, then crashed violently back down, bits and pieces of tile and mortar, brick and metal becoming deadly missiles as they sailed through the dust-filled air. The reporter ducked and so did the cameraman, each of them falling to the ground before the collapsing building. With the sound of terror filling the airwaves, the camera focused on the sidewalk for a only second, then the picture went blurry and finally totally black.

Jennifer began to scream.

CHAPTER SIXTEEN

THE LAST THOUGHT Beck had was of Jennifer.

Staring at the crazed man on the other side of the hallway, his hand clutching the package of explosives, his gaze wild and disoriented, Beck didn't think of the danger he was facing or even the imminent possibility of his own death. All he thought of was Jennifer. Brown eyes, chestnut hair, the face of an angel.

She was everything he'd always wanted in a woman and he'd never meet anyone else he could care for more.

But there would always be problems between the two of them. That was the nature of his work and nothing would change it. He couldn't tell her what he saw every day, even if he wanted to. It was too bloody, too violent, too horrible to share. Most of the time, he didn't even want to think of it himself.

She'd been right. They had no future...but not for the reasons she thought. The real truth was even more simple, as it usually was. They would never have a life together because he couldn't put her through that kind of agony—regardless of what she wanted. She deserved better. She deserved a husband who came home at night without blood on his clothes and death on his mind. She just deserved better.

A second later, Beck was flying through the air in silent agony, the blast stealing his hearing, a huge sliver of glass slicing him across the forehead. Pain radiated down his face and into his jaw, then the sting of blood hit his eyes. He landed with an excruciating thump, the air jarred from his lungs to be replaced by a searing heat.

He held on a moment more—long enough to feel the torture of a nearby flame, long enough to blink away the blood and see the fire—then the darkness came and Beck welcomed it.

"Is HE IN THERE? That's all I want to know! Just tell me if he's in there!"

Jennifer knew she sounded crazy, but she didn't care. Nothing mattered except for Beck. Lena McKinney stared at her with red-rimmed eyes and a harried expression. In one hand, she clutched a radio, in the other she held a handkerchief. As Jennifer watched, the woman brought the square of cloth up and swiped it over her face. Heat and flames were still coming from the building behind them, adding to the humidity and rising temperature of the early summer dawn.

"I can't tell you yet," she said. "All I can say is that we're working through the problem. Please get back behind the yellow tape, Miss Barclay, and as soon as we know something, I'll tell you, I promise.'' She turned and started to walk away.

"Wait—please! You don't understand,'' Jennifer cried. "I have to know. We're—''

The exhausted lieutenant stopped. Taking two steps back to where she'd been, she reached out and put her hand on Jennifer's arm, halting her flow of anguished words with a touch. "I *do* understand,'' she said in a level voice. Her gray stare held enough compassion to convince Jennifer. "I know how Beck feels about you, okay? And I'm guessing you feel the same way. I promise you, I will keep you informed.''

Miserably, Jennifer stood by and watched Lena hurry away. The scene was filled with chaos, fire trucks and police cars crowding every empty spot, people running in all directions. An arriving ambulance added to the confusion, its siren blaring, the red and blue lights on top streaking across the parking lot. Jennifer waited a moment longer, then she cursed and plunged into the disorder, running toward the ambulance without another thought.

They could arrest her if they wanted to, but she was going to find Beck first.

By the time she reached the ambulance, the two attendants had already leapt from the vehicle and dashed to the rear. Throwing open the doors, they pulled out various pieces of equipment then turned and jogged toward the building. Jennifer followed right behind them, dodging cops and firemen. The three of them reached the front door, or what was left of it, Jennifer already covered in a thin layer of soot and mist from the fire hoses still pointed toward the walls.

Nothing could have prepared her for the sight of the building's interior. As they entered the central atrium, the view to the south wasn't the wall that had been there, but the rear parking lot instead. The back of the building was completely gone. Bricks and drywall were crumpled up in piles of wet, soggy mounds, interspersed with shards of glass and metal. Electrical wires hung like snakes from what remained of the ceiling.

Jennifer's reaction was swift and immediate. In a flash, she was back at the school and seeing Howard's crumpled body. The men in black, the carnage, the whole horrible scene brought the taste of bile into her throat and up even farther. She could feel Juan's weight and smell the fear. For a moment, the feelings were overwhelming. She trembled under the onslaught and swayed, the nausea threatening to overtake her, blackness hovering on the edge of her vision.

Then with a strength she didn't know she had, she pushed through the images and breathed deeply. Three more breaths and they started to fade. Two more and they were gone.

But wasn't reality worse? She stared out over the

confusion with shock. No one could survive this kind of destruction and if Beck had been anywhere near... Fighting hysteria, she pushed the thought away and concentrated instead on the building. The corner that housed the beauty salon had taken the brunt of the explosion. One of the red leather chairs was upside down, its upholstery shredded. Another one had survived the blast, but was twisted where it sat. Two of the shampoo bowls had shattered along with all of the mirrors. An errant morning breeze fueled by an incongruent ray of sunshine came through an open hole where the roof had been hours before. A group of men, dressed in black, huddled near an overturned desk. One of them saw the ambulance attendants and cried out. ''Over here!''

His voice shook Jennifer out of her daze. She bulldozed past the two medics and ran toward the men, crying out as she went. ''Beck? Beck?''

The team looked up as one, but she didn't see their faces. All she saw was the figure they were surrounding, the man lying on the ground. He was covered in dirt, one leg at an impossible angle, his face a bloody pulp. His stillness told her the story; she didn't have to look longer to know he was dead.

She went weak then, her legs going out from beneath her, her stomach turning to water. Refusing to accept the truth her eyes were telling her, she cried out again, Beck's name sounding more like a moan than anything else.

She fell to her knees in the rubble just as one of the men stepped forward and spoke her name. His face was blackened, a horrible slash across one side of his forehead, a bloody handkerchief tied like a headband around it. She raised her stare to his, and only then—when she met the electric blue of his eyes—did she realize who he was.

For one stunned moment, they stared at each other, then Beck gathered her into his arms and she began to cry in earnest.

BECK WINCED as the medic cleaned the cut above his eye. Turning his head, he looked at Jennifer. Sitting beside him, inside the ambulance, she stared back, her face the color of the sheets on the gurney, her clothing black with soot. He wanted to scream at her for being there but he couldn't. He was too shocked by her appearance and the look in her eyes. If he didn't know any better, he might think she loved him.

But she didn't. She couldn't.

"That's enough." Beck growled at the attendant and shook his head away from the man's ministrations. "It'll be fine."

"I don't think so," he replied. "You need stitches. We'll transport you."

"Leave us alone." The eyes of the two men clashed under the glare of the lights in the vehicle, then the medic shrugged and disappeared. He wasn't going to argue. Beck turned to Jennifer. "You don't have any business here," he said bluntly. "It's too dangerous. How'd you even get inside anyway?"

"I followed the medics," she said. "No one noticed."

"Well, you shouldn't have. You could have been hurt."

She ignored his admonition. "The man...who was on the floor..."

"He's dead." Beck raised his hand to the bandage that covered one side of his forehead and winced. He spoke in short, clipped sentences, giving her the least amount of explanation he could. "He broke into the building to steal drugs then when the alarm went off and the beat cops came, it all went to hell. We couldn't reach him by phone because we didn't know where he was, and he didn't respond to the bullhorn. I went in with the team and when he saw us, he panicked. He grabbed something from that demolition office and set it off. At the very last minute, he pitched it toward the back of the building or there would have been less left of him than there was."

Her eyes took up half her face. "Why weren't you killed?"

"I was standing on the other side of the hallway because he wouldn't let me get any closer. I had two seconds' warning so I jumped behind a metal desk in the reception area. It took the brunt of the explosion and protected me when the ceiling fell in." He shook his head, then wished he hadn't. Pain rippled down his hairline and through his jaw. The aching stab wasn't as sharp as the one building inside his chest so he acted as if he didn't feel it. "Go home. You don't belong here."

His brusqueness didn't seem to faze her. "You aren't getting rid of me that easily, Beck. Don't even try."

He gave her a hostile look, but she didn't back down. She wasn't going to leave…so he had to. Pushing himself to the end of the stretcher, Beck threw his legs out the rear of the ambulance and stood. His surroundings shifted, so he closed his eyes and grabbed the handle of the door. When he opened his eyes again, Jennifer was beside him, gripping his arm and trying to steady him. It was like an ant holding up an elephant. In any other circumstances, he might have found it amusing.

He simply looked down at her. "Get out of here, Jennifer."

Her eyes took on a determined glint. "Look, I know we have our differences but when I got home and flipped on the television and saw this building…" Her throat moved as she swallowed, and in the light pouring from the van beside them, he could see her gaze begin to glimmer. "I—I—"

She was so beautiful, he couldn't stand it. He broke in before she could finish and before he could say something he'd regret. "Save it."

"Please, Beck. Just let me…."

"It's over, Jennifer." He softened his voice and lifted up one grimy hand to touch her face. Then he stopped. He was covered in blood and dirt and God only knew what else. Staring at his fingers, he shook his head. He couldn't let himself caress her. Or love her. What she'd said in his apartment, every word, was the truth, and the only truth there was. He couldn't share his job with her; she didn't need to hear about the violence and bloody gore. And she wanted to know everything about him. That was how she loved a person. There was only one way to resolve the problem.

He dropped his hand and stepped away from her. "Go home, Jennifer. Go home and take care of yourself and have a good life."

He memorized every detail of her face, then he walked away.

JENNIFER STOOD numbly in the parking lot and watched Beck leave. He couldn't do that, could he? Tell her just to go home and have a nice life? How could she if he wasn't going to be in it?

He went back into the blackened rubble of the building and she kept her eyes on him until he disappeared. Overhead, in the dawning pink-and-gold sky, a few white wispy clouds drifted by. They looked so peaceful against the still smoldering husk, the image didn't even make sense. Finally, she walked away, too.

"So THAT'S IT? You just left it at that?"

"There was nothing else *to* do." Jennifer glanced across the table at Wanda and shrugged. They were at AJ's, a local bar, and it was happy hour, but neither of them was very happy. Wanda obviously couldn't believe what she was hearing, and Jennifer was still in a state of shock. Four days had passed and she hadn't heard one word from Beck. And she wouldn't, she was sure. He'd been devastatingly clear about how he felt. He didn't want her around. Since then all she'd done was go back and forth between her apartment and Seacrest to visit her mother. Every day, hoping against hope, Jennifer had prayed Nadine would talk to her about Beck again, but her mother refused to emerge from the hazy confusion where she lived. The conversation they'd shared now seemed like a dream. Jennifer continued to talk to her, though, and drew some measure of comfort from it.

"Didn't you call him? Didn't you ask him?"

Interrupting Jennifer's thoughts, Wanda poked her straw in her drink with more energy than was needed. "The man must have had a good reason to send you packing...."

"Better than me telling him it'd never work out?" Jennifer shook her head miserably. "I think that was sufficient."

"But you changed your mind!"

"No, I didn't."

"Then why'd you go to the Renaissance Center?"

"I thought he was dead! I was terrified something had happened to him, and I had to go up there and see for myself. But no matter what, he's still going to lead that life and I can't stand it. The chaos, the confusion, the secrets. No way! I have dreams and that isn't one of them."

Wanda leaned back on her bar stool and nodded. "Yes, I can understand your point. You're obviously much, much happier now that he's not a part of your future. I can appreciate that, of course..."

Jennifer wanted to wail, but out of respect for the man on the stool next to her, she kept her voice low and moaned instead. "It doesn't matter one way or the other. He doesn't want me. He told me to go home and have a nice life. If that's not a kiss-off, then I don't know what is."

"He didn't mean it."

Reaching for her drink, Jennifer stopped, her hand still in the air. Wanda's words made her realize something she'd never thought of before, but thinking of it now, she knew how true it was. "Of course he means it. Beck doesn't say things he doesn't mean."

"Then you have to figure out why he said it."

"I think that's pretty obvious—"

"No, it's not." She leaned closer to the bar and then even closer to Jennifer. "The man loves you. You know that and I know that. Why would he tell you to go home and have a nice life?"

Jennifer couldn't get past the first few words. "He loves me? He's never said—"

"He didn't have to say it," Wanda answered impatiently.

"Then what makes you so sure he feels that way?"

"Think about it, Jennifer. You wouldn't sleep with a man you didn't love. And you wouldn't let yourself fall for him, unless it was safe. Safe as in 'he loves you, too.'" She held her hands out above the bar. "You love him. He loves you. All you need to do now is figure out why he pushed you away. Address that problem and everything's solved."

"There's more to it than that."

Wanda's dark eyes met Jennifer's. "There's always more when it comes to love. You just have to decide if it's worth the trouble or not."

"What about Howard?"

"What about him? You know Beck did the right thing, and you know he couldn't have told you all the details. You've understood that for a long time."

Wanda was right, and Jennifer nodded slowly. Seeing Beck walk out of that building had made her understand the point even better, though. Howard very well could have killed her or even worse, one of the children. He'd had a gun and he'd been irrational. Beck and his team had risked their lives to make sure that didn't happen, and all she'd done was question him. What on earth had made her think she'd known better?

She lifted her eyes and met Wanda's gaze. "You're right," she said simply. "But he doesn't want me now."

"So? Change his mind, if that's what you want. But do you really want it? I'm wondering because all I'm hearing are excuses." She put her hand on Jennifer's arm. "Are you just flat out scared?"

The question echoed in Jennifer's mind. Was she scared? The answer came swiftly.

She wasn't scared. She was terrified. All her life she'd searched for a calm and perfect life—what she thought was the opposite of her mother and father's marriage—and in the process she'd been pretty damn successful in keeping everything at bay, including love. But perfection didn't exist. Or did it? Wasn't Beck Winters as close as she'd ever found?

"You have to take a chance and go to him," Wanda said softly. "Tell him how you really feel. Tell him you love him. If he still doesn't want you, then you can accept that it's over. Otherwise, you'll always wonder if you tried hard enough."

JENNIFER MADE her way from the front of the station to the offices in the back. She was nervous and anxious, but Wanda, as usual, had delivered excellent advice. Jennifer had to give it her best shot otherwise she'd never know. She reached the office where she expected to see Beck, her hands wet and anxious, her chest so tight she could hardly breathe. But Lena was sitting at the desk, not Beck. The lieutenant looked momentarily nonplussed to see Jennifer, but she stood quickly and smiled. "Miss Barclay! How are you?"

"I'm fine," she answered nervously. "I was looking for Beck. I thought this was his office."

Lena's face took on an unexpected expression Jennifer couldn't decipher. "Well, it is…that is, it was." She stopped and shook her head. "Don't you know?"

A nervous flutter landed in Jennifer's stomach. "Know what?"

Lena hesitated then tilted her head to the chair beside the desk. "Why don't you sit down?"

Jennifer did as the woman suggested, a feeling of panic building up inside her. "Is everything okay? Beck's not hurt or…"

Lena looked puzzled. "He's fine, just fine, but I would have thought he'd tell you—"

"We had a fight," Jennifer said simply. "At the Renaissance Center the other day. He told me to leave, and I haven't spoken to him since."

"Oh, I'm sorry. I didn't know. I just assumed you two were…"

"I was. He wasn't."

Lena's gray eyes darkened sympathetically. "Men can be confusing, can't they? And now he's gone and done something even more unexpected and didn't even tell you."

"What?"

"He quit the team."

Jennifer's jaw actually dropped open in shock. "He what?"

"He left. Gave me his resignation last night. I really hate to lose him, but I'm not surprised." Lena fiddled with a pencil on her desk then sat back and looked at Jennifer. "He's the best man I've ever worked with, but we all have our limits, and he's reached his. It's better to leave before you cross that line."

Through her disbelief, Jennifer's curiosity rose. "Cross that line? What do mean?"

"Did he ever mention Randy Tamirisa?"

"The sniper..." Jennifer nodded. "He came to Beck's apartment a few nights ago—" She stopped and looked out the window of the office then back to Lena. "What's he got to do with all this?"

"He and Beck did not get along and I had to put Randy on probation. He went to Beck's place because he felt Beck had been behind his problem. The truth is, no one's behind his trouble but himself. Randy came to the line and didn't even know it. Thank goodness he's checked into a rehab center. They'll get him back on track." She looked regretful for a moment. "When your job takes over your life, you lose your perspective and when you lose that, you don't make good decisions. It's not important if you make widgets but if you're a cop and you have a gun in your hand, perspective is the only thing that keeps you alive."

"You think Beck was about to lose his?"

"I didn't, but he did."

"Why?"

Lena dropped the pencil and smiled softly. "Maybe you should turn around and ask him that question yourself."

SHE HAD ON a sleeveless dress, a lilac color, and her hair was piled up on top of her head with just a few strands hanging down around her face. He'd never seen Jennifer look more beautiful. And it broke his heart.

"Beck!" She spoke his name as she jumped to her feet.

He nodded but couldn't say much beyond her name. "Jennifer."

Lena rose as well, her gaze going from one to the other, before breaking the tension-filled silence. "I've got some work to do down the hall. If you two will excuse me…"

Lena eased around Beck, then disappeared into the hallway, softly closing the door behind her.

"What are you doing here, Jennifer?"

"I came to see you."

"Why?"

"Tell me first why you quit the team."

"I can't." He moved toward the chair Lena had vacated, but he didn't sit. He put his hands on the back of it and dug in, his fingers indenting the cracked and frayed leather.

"Can't or won't?"

"Does it matter?"

"It does to me."

He sat down, the springs of the leather desk chair creaking as they took his weight. "I don't really know," he answered, the truth hurting as he verbalized it for the very first time. "I just felt it was something I needed to do."

"Did I have anything to do with that decision?"

Did she? He lost himself for a moment in her eyes, then he shook his head. He'd told her the truth; he wasn't really sure why he'd chosen to leave, but it'd felt right and for once, he'd simply done what he thought he should without questioning his motives. "I decided this on my own...." he answered. "But maybe you did."

She looked puzzled, then he continued, the reasons forming only as the words took shape. "I think I just decided it was time to move on," he said thoughtfully. "We all reach a point in our life, if we're smart, when we know it's best to change gears. I don't want to be one of those old cops who can't turn loose of the badge. You see them in the coffee shops, still telling their tales, pretending it all still matters. There's got to be more to life than that but I won't know unless I look for it." He shook his head. "Maybe I'll come back and maybe I won't. I don't know yet, but I do know it's time for a break. You made me realize that and I guess I should thank you.''

He leaned back and stared at her. ''So that's my sad story. You tell me why you're here now.''

She moved around and took the chair beside the desk. Folding her hands she placed them in her lap, then she looked up at him and took a deep breath. ''The reason I'm here is that...'' She faltered, her tongue slipping out to moisten her lips. ''I wanted to tell you I think I was wrong. I understand now why you did some of the things you did. And why you couldn't tell me everything. I'm sorry I was so dense before.''

The cold spot that had been inside his heart since he'd turned her away suddenly began to warm. He shut down the process. This wasn't what he thought it was, he warned himself.

''All my life I've wanted straight lines and written rules. I wanted schedules and order and bells to tell me when to do things. Instead of leaving myself open to new possibilities, I've closed doors. That was wrong and I've come to realize why.'' She stood up to move closer to him. When he saw the look in her eyes, he rose, too.

She tilted her head back and stared at him. ''I was scared...and I still am. But I love you, Beck. And that means accepting you and your life as it is, tumultuous or not. You were right when you said I'm living in the past. My parents' mistakes don't have to be mine and they definitely aren't yours. I've known that all along, but knowing the truth and accepting it are two different things.''

Stunned into silence, all Beck could do was gaze down at her. It seemed impossible that this was happening.

Starting to say so, he reached out for her and put his hands on her shoulders. She was trembling.

''I really do love you,'' she said before he could speak. ''Do you think there's any possibility—''

''I love you, too,'' he said roughly. ''I've loved you from the minute I saw you inside that school. You were so brave and so beautiful I couldn't believe it. Without even knowing what kind of woman you were, I knew I loved you, right then and there.''

She reached up and gripped his hands, her hold ferocious, her expression fierce. ''Then why didn't you tell me? Why did you send me away the other night?''

''I sent you away because I believe you should get what you want...and more. You, out of every woman I've ever met, deserve a husband who can come home every night, physically and mentally. I wasn't sure I could give you that, and I wanted it for you as much as you wanted it for yourself.''

Her eyes filled with tears and they spilled over. ''I want *you*,'' she said simply. ''You're that man, whether you fit the description or not, it doesn't matter. The only thing that counts is whether or not you want me, too.''

He crushed her to him in a hug that stole their breaths. ''I've never wanted anything else.'' He pulled back so he could look at her. ''Will you marry me, Jennifer?''

She smiled through her tears. ''You name the day and I'll pick the place.''

EPILOGUE

SEACREST HAD NEVER looked lovelier. In the late-evening breeze, the water off the bay rippled with small whitecaps. Several rows of folding chairs had been lined up and down a bright-red carpet leading out from the nearby gazebo. Betty and her husband, all the teachers and the entire Emerald Coast SWAT team, both cells, were sitting and chatting. Someone had threaded white satin ribbons and small pink roses through the fretwork of the gazebo, and as Jennifer stared at their fluttering ends and soft petals, she knew who. Wanda. The nurse stood expectantly at the entrance of the gazebo and smiled back at Jennifer. Beside her, in a gleaming wheelchair, Nadine waved gaily in her direction as well.

Jennifer felt her throat close up. The last thing her mother had asked before they'd wheeled her toward the minister waiting to lead the vows was "Where's Danny?"

"He's watching from the back, Mom," she'd answered. "I saw him just a while ago."

"Oh, good!" Nadine had smiled, her soft, fragile

skin even more translucent in the late summer sun. "I'll see him later."

"Absolutely," Jennifer had said.

She put the thought where it belonged and turned her eyes to Beck. Standing on the other side of the carpet from Wanda, he looked back at Jennifer and smiled. Then he held out his hand and she began to walk toward him.

*Being on the SWAT team is hard enough.
Imagine being in charge. Watch for
Lieutenant Lena McKinney's story—*

THE COMMANDER

—coming in August 2002

*Now turn the page
for an exciting preview…*

The Commander
by
Kay David

Somewhere off the coast of Cuba

THERE WAS no moon, thank God.

Andres Casimiro stared into the endless black of the water and counted the only blessing he had. If there'd been light, he'd be a dead man by now.

Easing the throttle of the boat, he slowed the vessel and cut the engine. The gentle sound of slapping waves replaced the throb of the motor, and he took a breath of something that felt like relief. No light, no noise…he might have a chance. In the still, hot quiet, he looked down at the chart on the table beside the wheel. He was in the right spot, too. All he had to do now was wait.

And think.

Andres had never been a patient man, but in this instance, the waiting would be easier than the thinking. He *had* to make his mind as empty as the sea beneath him to get through this. If he couldn't, the next few hours would be his last.

The minutes ticked by slowly. After a while, he

lowered his arm to hide the light and pressed his watch to read the dial—1:00 a.m. Despite his best efforts to the contrary, a surge of disappointment—so strong it felt more like grief—washed over him. He and Lena would have been in Cancun by now, the wedding ceremony long behind them, the "I do's" said and sealed with a kiss. They would be settling into the villa on the beach. He'd reserved the last one on the Point, where no one ever came. He'd wanted the privacy, the intimacy of it. When he'd told Lena about the special house, she'd smiled in that secret way of hers and said one word. "Perfect."

He wondered what one word she had for him right now. It wasn't *perfect,* he was sure.

A tiny beam broke the darkness, its unexpected radiance brilliant against the inky night before it winked out. Andres's heart bucked as if someone had punched him, and he fumbled the flashlight he'd been holding, dropping it to the deck. With a curse, he fell to his knees and patted the wooden planks. His fingers found the flashlight and he jumped up and flicked it once, then again. He thought he heard a splash, but he wasn't sure.

He started the countdown in his mind. They'd agreed on every thirty seconds. *One thousand one,* he began silently, *one thousand two…*

The numbers echoed in his mind, each digit accompanied by the same mantra. Forgive me, Lena. I didn't have a choice…. Forgive me…

He'd been completely unprepared for the phone call he'd gotten early that morning. Mateo's voice, coming over the tinny line, was the last one Andres had expected to hear only a few hours before his wedding. His best friend, Mateo Aznar, had helped the eighteen-year-old Andres escape Cuba twenty-one years before and had served since as the sole source of information Andres had on the island. A former cop but now working for the Justice Department, Andres passed the intelligence on, most of it centering on one organization—the Red Tide. A terrorist group backed by drug sales, they had no good intentions.

"You've got to come," Mateo had gasped over the phone. "They've found out about everything. The radio, the lines, everything. If you can't get me out, they'll kill me."

Andres's breath had stopped. "But how did they—?"

"I have my suspicions."

"The same as mine?"

They hadn't wanted to say the name—in Cuba, there were ears everywhere. Andres wasn't sure Destin was any better.

"*Sí,*" Mateo had replied. "I'm certain it's him."

"Do you have any proof?"

"I've got records of the payments. I think it's good enough together with what you know of his 'friends.'"

They'd gone on to what was needed, talking in a

code they'd already developed. Within hours, Andres had been on a plane to Miami, then at the dock, renting the boat. He loved Lena desperately and the decision had torn him apart. But it was the only one he could make. When this was all over, he'd go back to her. He'd tell her what he could and pray she'd understand. Deep down, he knew she wouldn't, but to get through the night, he had to believe in the lie.

One thousand twenty-nine, one thousand thirty… Holding the flashlight above his head, Andres switched it on, the bright flame burning like a falling star. His eyes searched the water. He'd anchored well offshore, but Mateo should have been visible by now. A movement to the right caught Andres's eye. Was it him? His palms pressing into the railing, Andres peered over the side of the boat.

If he hadn't been so focused, he might have seen them.

As it was, when the white-hot flash of the spotlight blinded him, Andres was astonished. The huge cutter loomed suddenly as if the boat had been dropped from above. After his vision returned, shocked and in a panic, Andres shot his gaze back to the water. Twenty yards off the bow of his own vessel, he spotted Mateo, floundered in the waves. Before he could cry out, the larger boat angled itself between the two men.

"Put your hands up and prepare to be boarded. Drop any weapons now!" The warning was given in

Spanish, through a bullhorn from the deck of the ship. *"¿Comprende?"*

Instead of answering, Andres screamed into the night. "Hurry, Mateo, hurry! You can make it! Swim faster! I'll get you!" He revved the engine and within seconds, he maneuvered the tiny boat around the cutter and headed back toward his friend.

The water was choppy and rough but Andres would never forget the look on his friend's face as their eyes connected. In that instant, that split second, he knew he'd done the right thing. Leaving Lena at the altar, giving up the only woman he'd ever loved...how could he have lived with himself otherwise?

Andres reached Mateo just as an onslaught of bullets peppered the water, a steady stream of fire and death. A searing pain streaked down Andres's arm as he took a direct hit, but the wound was nothing to the agony he felt as Mateo screamed and began to flail about in the suddenly crimson waves.

"Goddammit, no! No!" Andres gunned the boat and cut past the spot, turning the craft as tightly as he dared to fly back once more. He searched the waves with desperate eyes, placing himself between the huge ship and where Mateo had been, but there was nothing to see.

Mateo was gone.

Andres screamed a useless curse, then he spun the boat around and disappeared into the darkness. Gunfire followed his wake, but it couldn't reach him. His craft was fast and small, and the cutter didn't have a chance.

He made it to Miami a few hours later. He'd sacrificed love for loyalty, a wife for a friend.

Now he had neither. It'd take him a lifetime to forget.

And forever to forgive.

* * *

Remember, The Commander *is an August 2002 Silhouette Superromance. So look for it next month.*

SILHOUETTE® SUPERROMANCE™

AVAILABLE FROM 19TH JULY 2002

THE WRONG BROTHER Bonnie K Winn

Twins

Paul Elliott has to find his identical twin brother's murderer—even if it means covering up Matthew's death and assuming his identity. Paul hopes that Katherine, Matthew's wife, is guilty because, if not, then he's deceiving an innocent woman he's beginning to love.

THE COMMANDER Kay David

The Guardians

Two years ago, Lena tried to be both a woman and a cop—it didn't work out. Now her ex-fiancé is back and her SWAT team is assigned to protect him. Lena wants to walk away but she'll do her duty, keeping her true feelings buried. But that's *before* the shots are fired…

BIRTHRIGHT Judith Arnold

Riverbend

Aaron Mazerik isn't the town bad boy anymore, but some people still don't think he's good enough—especially not for golden girl, Lily Holden. Which is fine with Aaron, since he's convinced there's an even bigger reason he and Lily shouldn't be together…

THE FAMILY WAY Rebecca Winters

9 Months Later

Pregnant, widowed, single mother of two Wendy Sloan didn't know what to make of handsome stranger Josh Walker. He appeared too good to be true—fixing up the place, looking far too attractive, and wanting to be a father to her children… What's a woman to do?

MARIE FERRARELLA
BEVERLY BARTON
LINDSAY McKENNA
DANGEROUS TO LOVE
3 SENSATIONAL, SEXY ROMANCES!
On sale 21st June 2002
0702/81/SH32

SILHOUETTE® SUPERROMANCE™

is proud to present

Friends... Lovers... Strangers...
These couples' lives are about to change
radically as they become parents-to-be

AND BABY MAKES SIX
Linda Markowiak
May

THE FRAUDULENT FIANCÉE
Muriel Jensen
June

SNOW BABY
Brenda Novak
July

THE FAMILY WAY
Rebecca Winters
August

Join us every month throughout the
whole of 2002 for one of these dramatic,
involving, emotional books.

0502/SH/LC29

SILHOUETTE® SUPERROMANCE™

Welcomes you to

RIVERBEND

*Riverbend... the kind of place where everyone
knows your name — and your business.
Riverbend... home of a group of small-
town sons and daughters who've
been friends since school.*

*They're all grown up now. Living their
lives and learning that you can get through
anything as long as you have your friends.*

Five wonderful stories:

0802/SH/LC37

2 FREE

books and a surprise gift!

We would like to take this opportunity to thank you for reading this Silhouette® book by offering you the chance to take TWO more specially selected titles from the Superromance™ series absolutely FREE! We're also making this offer to introduce you to the benefits of the Reader Service™—

- ★ FREE home delivery
- ★ FREE gifts and competitions
- ★ FREE monthly Newsletter
- ★ Exclusive Reader Service discount
- ★ Books available before they're in the shops

Accepting these FREE books and gift places you under no obligation to buy, you may cancel at any time, even after receiving your free shipment. Simply complete your details below and return the entire page to the address below. **You don't even need a stamp!**

YES! Please send me 2 free Superromance books and a surprise gift. I understand that unless you hear from me, I will receive 4 superb new titles every month for just £3.49 each, postage and packing free. I am under no obligation to purchase any books and may cancel my subscription at any time. The free books and gift will be mine to keep in any case.

U2ZEA

Ms/Mrs/Miss/Mr ....Initials...............................
BLOCK CAPITALS PLEASE

Surname ....

Address ....

....

....Postcode...................................

Send this whole page to:
UK: FREEPOST CN81, Croydon, CR9 3WZ
EIRE: PO Box 4546, Kilcock, County Kildare (stamp required)